REVOLUTIONS
OF THE HEART

REVOLUTIONS
OF THE HEART

Marsha Qualey

Houghton Mifflin Company
Boston

Library of Congress Cataloging-in-Publication Data

Qualey, Marsha.
  Revolutions of the heart / Marsha Qualey.
     p.   cm.
  Summary: Cory's seventeenth year is marked by her mother's sudden
death, the return of her hotheaded older brother, her romance with a
Native American boy, and the eruption of bigotry in her small
Wisconsin town.
  ISBN 0-395-64168-3
  [1. Family problems — Fiction.   2. Indians of North America —
Fiction.   3. Prejudices — Fiction.   4. Wisconsin — Fiction.]
I. Title.
PZ7.Q17N1   1993   92-24528
[Fic] — dc20   CIP
                        AC

Printed in the United States of America

QUM   10   9   8   7   6   5

I would like to acknowledge the help of Sarah Hanna; Marilyn O'Brien; Nanette Missaghi; Dave Qualey; and, above all, my editor, Laura Hornik.

For my children—
Laura, Ellen, Jane, and Ben.
Brilliant stars.

1

CORY KNUTSON gave the volume knob on the radio a good crank, lifted the vacuum hose up to her face, gripped it with both hands, and sang into the brush attachment: ". . . home of the brave." She punched the air with a fist and took a bow as the stadium crowd cheered for Whitney.

She turned off the radio. Most of her friends just hated Whitney Houston. Cory often accused them of listening only to music by bone-thin guys wearing extremely tight pants. She, however, had always liked listening to the kind of singers her mother called "babes with big voices." Liked them, maybe, because she couldn't sing at all — couldn't even carry a tune in a bucket, her mother once observed. But Cory sang anyway, especially in the motel rooms while she cleaned.

Singing was a way to pass the time and amuse herself while she did the tedious motel chores. Change the sheets, scour the toilet, vacuum the carpet, clean, clean, clean. Bored as she got on her five-hour weekend shifts, Cory still had to admit that it wasn't the world's worst job, not by far.

She yanked the vacuum cord out of the outlet, pressed a button on the canister with her toe, and the cord was quickly reeled in. "Slaughtering pigs," she said to herself. "That would be the worst." Her stepfather's uncle had retired the previous summer after forty years of working in the hog kill in a meatpacking plant in Minnesota. Shortly thereafter he had visited them at their home in northern Wisconsin, and every day, four times a day, had gone swimming in the lake behind their house. Even when he was soaking wet with the clean, cold lake water, Cory had imagined she could smell the stench of the hog kill.

"The worst," she said firmly. She sniffed her hands and made a face. She had her own occupational aroma: cleanser and dust. No matter how thoroughly she showered and soaped and perfumed, she was certain the odor of her work was embedded in the pores of her hands.

But all in all, it was not a bad job. Especially when there weren't that many employment options, not in a small town like Summer, not for someone whose parents wouldn't let her work on school nights. Not many options at all for a seventeen-year-old with a five-hundred-dollar debt.

Cory collected her rags and cans of cleansers and dumped them into a pail. She gave the room a once-over, knowing it would be perfect even though she had rushed. The guests had departed late, and she had stayed to clean the room.

"I am the best," she said, snapping her fingers. The bathroom sparkled and the bedding was taut. The dresser was dusted and gleaming, with only the Bible left on its polished surface. Recently, Cory had started picking out Bible verses and setting the ribbon marker to open onto some of the good passages, the ones she and her Sunday school classmates had giggled and moaned over outside of class, the passages about illicit sex or gruesome violence or ceaseless begetting. Today she had marked all the Bibles at Judges 4:21. Death by tent peg driven through the skull.

The room passed her inspection, and she slipped the pail handle over her arm and pulled the vacuum toward the door. She grimaced as she reached the large mirror that was bolted onto the wall. After six hours of room cleaning she didn't need a mirror to remind her that she looked like the floor of a New York City cab. Not that she had ever been in a New York City cab. Not that she had ever been in New York City. Not that I've ever been anywhere, she thought. Cory appraised the image. She hated the height (five two); admired the figure (soft only where it should be); made plans for the straight brown hair and face (a perm, a black rinse, a trip to the dermatologist).

She blew a kiss to the girl in the mirror and left the room. Wind blasted across the motel parking lot and tossed up snow in her face. She loaded her equipment onto the maid's cart, lowered her head, and pushed the cart along the concrete walk that ran the length of the motel. In the office, Mr. Bartleby was checking in a guest and nodded to her as she wrestled the cart through the door and around the front counter.

"All done, Cory?"

"You can call the health inspector."

Mr. Bartleby handed a key to the guest. "Number Twenty-two. Out the door, go to your left, upstairs." The man departed, and the motel owner turned to Cory. "Thanks for staying late."

"I get paid extra, right?"

"Right. One hour, time and a half." He looked out the front window. "I wish that snow would come down harder and bring in a few nervous travelers. I love a good Saturday blizzard."

Cory watched his hand stroke up and down his massive belly. She wondered what such a huge stomach could look like bare. Maybe just like an enlarged version of the man's round, pasty, bald head. She decided it was probably too gross for words and hoped she would never see Mr. Bartleby in a swimsuit. Or in nothing at all. She couldn't imagine how his wife enjoyed sex, or how they even did it.

"Are you going to the basketball game tonight?"

Cory looked directly at his smiling face and had a terrible thought: What if he could read minds? She breathed deeply and tried to clear hers.

"Is something wrong, Cory? Do you feel faint?" He shook his head. "You and your mother. I saw her the other day at the IGA and she looked terrible. Of course, if Mike is doing the cooking these days . . ."

"I'm fine."

"Going to the game?"

"No."

He smiled. "Still in prison?"

"That's a fair description of my life."

"Cory, you can't blame your parents. You put a nice big hole in Dawn's store window. My oldest girl —"

The phone rang and Cory was saved from once again hearing about his daughter's string of auto accidents. Mr. Bartleby was a talker and hard to escape. As he addressed the phone, she quickly pushed the cart into the private room behind the counter and unlocked the maid's closet. She could hear the conversation and sensed that it wouldn't go on long. She wanted to get away before her boss again claimed her as an audience.

Yes, she had put a nice big hole in the front window of Dawn Remer's Country Store. And yes, she was still grounded, restricted from anything resembling fun. Prison, the cheerful man liked to call it. Ha ha.

But the whole town knew she was in a social prison, knew that Cory Knutson had sneaked out one night in her stepfather's new pickup after her mother and stepfather had said, "No, the weather is too bad and you may not drive to town." *They* had left then (in the same bad weather, Cory had pointed out) in her mother's car to visit friends.

Bored and thirsty, Cory had reasoned to herself that a half-mile trip to Dawn's store wasn't the same as driving five miles to town. She left to get a soda.

She hadn't guessed there would be ice under a large patch of snow in the store's parking lot; therefore, when she braked hard and braked fast just as she was reaching across the seat for another cassette tape, the truck went left, went right, turned around, and slammed its backside into the store window. No one was hurt, but the truck lost a taillight, the window was smashed and spread everywhere, and Dawn's stock of magazines and romance novels was ripped and smeared with glass and grime. The damage was covered by insurance, except for the five-hundred-dollar deductible. Cory's parents paid that but demanded that she pay them back.

So Cory found a job at Bartleby's Inn. After the first weekend of work, she'd decided the worst thing, the cruelest part, wasn't the job, or the debt, or maybe even the grounding. But she had also lost her driving privileges, and that hurt. She loved driving — loved the movement, loved the liberty. Ever since she had passed her driver's test and got her license, Cory had been on wheels. She drove to town, drove friends to basketball games, drove for groceries, drove anywhere. She always drove with music on. Singing, seat dancing, pounding the beat on the steering wheel, she drove to the limits of her world.

But for the last three weeks her keys and her license had been locked in a drawer in her parents' desk.

"Extreme cruelty," Cory muttered, then gave the maid's cart an angry push and it rolled into the closet and slammed against the wall. Loose items rearranged themselves noisily. She emptied the dirty linen into the laundry bin, grabbed her jacket off a hook, nudged the door closed with her foot, and ran through the office just as Mr. Bartleby was saying good-bye.

"I'm done," she said firmly. "See you tomorrow." She was out.

She didn't stop to put on her coat for nearly half a block and didn't realize until she raised her arm to push it into the quilted sleeve that she was still holding the ring of motel keys. She froze while considering the gruesome thought of listening to her boss tell another lengthy family story, and for a full minute she stood in the blowing snow along Main Street, Highway 8, dangling several keys from a silver ring looped over her outstretched hand.

A car horn blasted, and she breathed again. As she watched it pull over, she dropped the key ring into her pocket. Mr. Bartleby had his own set; she wouldn't go back.

Tony Merrill waved her into the car, and as she pulled the car door closed she shivered with the first realization of how cold it was.

"Hey, old man," she said. "Thanks. It's cold." Tony was a classmate and lifelong friend. They had even dated a few times the previous year until he had been blindsided by a ferocious love for a new girl in town, Sasha Hunter. Fortunately for Tony, Sasha was likewise afflicted, and they had been together since. Cory hadn't minded, since Sasha had become a good friend.

"You shouldn't hitchhike."

"I wasn't."

"Standing by the side of the road with your arm out?"

"I was thinking."

"That's a first." He sniffed. "Nice perfume. What is it, Bleach 'n' Bath?"

"Really. I've been working. Know what that is?"

"No comment."

Cory leaned, twisted, and wiggled into her coat. She twice accidentally socked Tony on the arm as she maneuvered in the small space.

"I'm beginning to regret this simple act of kindness," he said after she hit him the second time.

"Sorry. I left the motel in a hurry. Tony, could you drop me off at the nursing home? I have to meet my mother."

He nodded and turned the car back onto the road. "Going to the game tonight?"

"No."

"Still grounded? Well, it was a pretty big hole."

Cory looked out the window. "I think I've had this conversation before, maybe in a bad dream."

"When is your release?"

"One more week."

Tony honked at some classmates who were loitering in the cold outside of Zanker's service station. "Could you sneak out and go with Sash and me?"

"Only if I have a death wish. Anyway, you know how I love being a third wheel with you guys."

He pulled into the nursing home parking lot. "There sure are a lot of cars. Is it visiting hours?"

"Oh, no," Cory groaned. "I forgot they were having a wine and cheese party for the residents. The head nurse is leaving."

"I'll take you home."

"It has to be almost over. And I can't go home because Mom and I had plans."

"Saturday night with your mother? What fun did you have in mind, a Disney movie?"

Cory closed one hand over another and sat still. She wasn't sure she wanted to tell him. Bad enough that she was spending Saturday night with her mother. She watched as a crooked, white-haired lady waved from the door of the home to her departing guests. The woman continued waving long after the car had driven away. Cory turned to Tony.

"Do you want to know the god-awful truth?"

"Sure."

"We're going to a powwow."

Tony was usually quick with a joke or a sharp remark, and Cory waited for it now. He surprised her.

"The one at the armory in Twin Lakes? Sash wanted to go."

"She did?"

He shrugged off her disbelief. "She's real curious about things. I told her, though, that the Indian stuff around here is all part of a different world. She called me a cute bigot. I'm not a bigot. It's just not my world, and I don't want to go gawk at a bunch of people dressed weird and dancing in a circle. Why are you and your mom going?"

"To gawk, I guess. One of the women she works with is sort of a friend and she invited us. My mother accepted."

Tony combed his fingers through his chin-length

blond hair, which was straight and usually hanging over half of his face, a style nearly identical to Cory's. Tony's mother ran the town's only hair salon and whenever she was enthusiastic about a new look or cut it showed up on any number of townspeople, regardless of gender.

Tony's hair fell back down over his left eye. "After Sash called me a bigot, she said it would be a good idea to have some school programs on cultural understanding."

"Like what?"

"You'll have to ask her. She's full of ideas. She said . . ." He stroked the bumpy ridge on the underside of the steering wheel with his thumb.

"Said what?" Cory prompted.

"That since you were one of the junior reps to the student council maybe you would bring up some proposals. She'd write them."

"When did she start cooking up all this?"

He shook his head. "Beats me. I warned you, okay?"

"You should keep her busier, Tony."

"Hey, I try, but I can't keep the lights off all the time."

Cory feigned disgust and punched him on the arm. "Ow," he said. "That's three times. You're out of here."

Cory stood and watched as he drove away too quickly. Tony's car swerved as he turned onto the street, and he almost swiped a lamppost. He regained control and disappeared around a corner.

Just inside the nursing home front door several residents were clustered, looking at the ground and laughing. Then they looked up and at each other, and the laughter increased until each of them seemed in danger of shaking apart. One of them noticed Cory.

"Here's Margaret's girl. Tell her what you did, Alicia." A pudgy hand with several rings permanently embedded in the fingers clamped onto Cory's arm with surprising strength. "Tell her, Alicia!"

Cory smiled at Alicia, who was one of the residents she knew best. Alicia was tall and towered over Cory. She leaned forward, and her long black hair fell around her pale face. Cory could think only of countless fairy-tale illustrations of wicked witches.

"My shoes," Alicia began, articulating each word so clearly it seemed to pop out of her glossy, purple lips. "My shoes don't match!" This was a signal for renewed laughter among her companions, which quickly dissipated into six simultaneous anecdotes about personal lapses of one sort or another. Cory squeezed Alicia's hand and slipped away.

She sometimes stopped to visit with the residents when she came to get a ride with her mother after school or work. She was usually willing to listen to someone's life story or admire a display of family pictures, but the encounters often drained her. She wondered frequently how her mother and the other nurses could sustain the energy needed to work at the home.

Her mother hadn't managed today. Cory could tell immediately when she entered the staff lounge. Her

11

mother was stretched out on the sofa, feet stacked heel-to-toe, eyes closed.

"What's wrong, Mom?"

Margaret Knutson turned her face slowly and Cory gasped. Her mother was as pale as Alicia.

"What's wrong?" she repeated.

"Nothing." Her mother sat up. "I'm just tired. Nothing's wrong."

"I'll tell you what's wrong," a voice said firmly.

Cory turned and smiled at Roxanne Chapelle, one of her mother's coworkers. Roxanne eased around Cory and dropped a box on the cluttered coffee table. Cory heard the muffled tinkling of metal on metal.

"What's wrong is your mother hasn't been taking her iron pills, she skips lunch daily, and today she worked an extra two hours cleaning up after the party." She offered a steaming cup to her friend. "Soup. Not the soda you wanted."

Margaret smiled at her daughter. "She doesn't approve of my diet."

Roxanne motioned to Cory to sit on one of the chairs. "I'm so glad you're coming with us tonight."

Cory nodded slightly. She knew better than even to hint there had been no choice.

Roxanne lifted the cover off the box she had set on the table. "I present the world's most beautiful jingle dress." Almost before Cory could wonder what a jingle dress was, she had her answer.

The short-sleeved dress was a bright blue that made her think of indigo buntings flashing between branches in the trees around her house. There were hundreds of small metal cones sewn onto the fabric in tidy rows. Roxanne shook the dress slightly, and the cones chimed as they bounced against each other. A jingle dress.

"Perfect, isn't it?" said Roxanne. "And your mother helped."

"Helped make a dress?" Cory's impolite disbelief amused the women.

"Helped with the jingles. They're made of tobacco can lids. Before she made Mike quit chewing she saved all his can lids. Look closely and you can tell that's what they are."

Cory obediently fingered one of the thin cones. "I wouldn't have guessed."

"We Indians are resourceful." Cory didn't know if she should laugh; Roxanne joked a lot. She settled on a slight smile.

"It's Paula's first fancy dress," said Roxanne. "If we don't get going, we won't make it to Twin Lakes in time for the grand entry, and then I will be one sorry mother." She folded the dress, placed it in the box, and set down the cover. "Margaret, are you sure you're up to this?"

"Your soup has worked a miracle, Rox. I could run a marathon. Anyway, Cory can drive —"

"Yes!" cheered Cory.

"Just tonight, dear."

"My license, I don't have my license. Some cruel people took it away."

"I brought it. It's in my purse and it stays there."

"Mom, please."

13

"Hey, Cory," said Roxanne. "I saw that hole in Dawn's store. Big hole, big probation."

"Everyone saw the hole. Everyone for miles around."

"Cory can drive," Margaret continued, "and we can sit in the back, Rox, and you can tell me everything about powwows."

Roxanne nodded. "The first thing you should know is that they start with a blood initiation involving select male virgins. Then —"

"Roxanne."

Roxanne lifted two jackets from hooks on a wall and handed one to Margaret with a smile. "I'm just so glad you both agreed to come tonight."

Cory followed the women out the door and into the hall. Spotting a clock on the wall, she zipped up her jacket with a defiant yank. All her friends would be leaving soon for the game in Rhinelander while she, Cory Knutson, the town's most famous driver, was going to a powwow.

2

EIGHT HUNDRED people lived year-round in Summer, Wisconsin, and most of them knew Cory Knutson. Or knew her family, or knew someone who worked with her mother or with Mike at the window factory, or had gone to high school with her brother, Rob, or was related somehow to Mike's ex-wife. Most people knew the story of her father's death in a hunting accident. Cory had been three when he died and seven when her mother married Mike. A year later Mike adopted Cory and she took his last name. But Rob, who was seven years older and could still remember and love his father, didn't want that change. So, until last year when he married and moved to southern Wisconsin to work on the state road crews, there were two names on the mailbox — Kranz and Knutson.

That was the family history, and, just as the people of Summer knew it all, Cory knew theirs. She knew

15

about the deaths, the romances, the church affiliations, the school problems, the babies, the new cars. She knew something about everyone.

Almost everyone, she admitted now. Eyeing Roxanne in the rearview mirror and listening to the women share an animated, girlish conversation, Cory realized she couldn't say she knew very much about any of the American Indians who lived around town, or the few who were in school. She could count on two hands the Indian students in any of her classes and could picture them sitting at their own table in the lunchroom. The Reservation, some of the kids called it. Always the same table, right next to the one she always shared with Tony and Sasha and Karin and the others. Tables side by side, every noon. Throughout any day there were never more than a few words exchanged; however, at least there were never any bad ones.

Not like in Ashland or Hayward, larger towns near the reservations. Cory knew that in those places bad feelings often boiled and spilled over into real nastiness. She had heard from Mike's youngest child who lived in Ashland with her mother that there were plenty of fights in and out of school and plenty of tire-slashing and name-calling.

But in Summer it had always been calm just living side by side. A different world, Tony had said. A parallel dimension, Cory added to herself as she recalled a science fiction movie she had recently watched. And apart from visits exchanged with Roxanne, or Peter Rosebear, who worked with Mike and sometimes came by on Fridays for an end-of-the-week beer, her family, like others, didn't mix. There was distance, but anyone would have to believe it was caused by habit, not hate.

Cory parked the car at the edge of the crowded armory lot. Roxanne opened the door, and Cory could hear drums. People streamed into the cavernous building's open doors, as though drawn by the relentless pounding. A parallel dimension, and she suspected she had just crossed over.

"This is a competition powwow," said Roxanne as she led them to the armory. "There's some good prize money, and there will be dancers and drum groups from all over."

Roxanne seemed to know everyone, but after stopping a few times to introduce her guests, she gave up. "This is no good," she said. "We'll never get in at this rate, and Paula is probably already frantic. Do you mind if we meet people later?"

Margaret laughed and pushed her friend forward. "Your rudeness is just barely forgivable."

Once inside, their progress was slowed by a seemingly impenetrable mass of people. Looking around, Cory twice came face-to-face with young men in full regalia: feathers, beads, face paint.

Not war paint. She willed herself not to think of it as war paint. And the drum — she didn't know if it was actually called a tom-tom. The drum song had intensified in volume and rhythm, and she could feel her heartbeat adjust its pace. She saw several dancers in traditional dress: a man wearing a huge feathered bustle, two girls in fringed buckskin and beaded ribbons, women with elaborate and colorful shawls. Then, stepping at last into the main hall and seeing a sea of men and women and boys and girls in fantastic, puzzling, beautiful dress, Cory knew she would be content to be quiet and watch.

Roxanne dropped her nylon bowling jacket on a folding chair. "Let's take these seats. I told Paula to find me by the host drum, and that's these boys here." She waved at a group of men sitting around a large kettle drum. Several of them raised drumsticks in response. Cory dropped her own coat on a chair and looked around the room. Rows of chairs had been set up on two sides of the hall. At each of the open ends there were two drum groups. One of the circles at the far end was drumming and singing. Cory watched the rhythmic action of the rising and falling arms and she was mesmerized by the white-tipped sticks, which caught the glare of the fluorescent ceiling lights as they streaked up and down.

"Mother, where the hell have you been?"

Cory, attention diverted from the drum, swallowed a smile as Paula pounded Roxanne on the shoulder. Evidently mother-daughter exasperation was universal among the races.

Roxanne handed her daughter the box she had guarded as a treasure. "You have time."

"Right. Ten minutes." Paula took the box and flipped a wave to her mother's guests. "Glad you came, meet you later." She pushed past a few people and disappeared into the crowd.

18

The persistent drumming was lulling, and Cory again focused on the rhythm. A different drum began its song, and she shifted her attention to it, away from Roxanne, who was introducing friends and relations to Margaret. All around her, there was talk of road conditions, the weather, jobs, tribal politics, and the winter's new babies. Most of the talk spilled into a single, nonsensical stream of voices punctuated occasionally by the familiar sound of her mother's laugh.

People were lining up between two of the drum circles. Cory guessed they were preparing for what Roxanne had called the grand entry. A microphone crackled, catching the attention of the crowd and sending a signal to the drum to stop. It crackled again, then cleared, and a deep voice boomed out a welcome. After several minutes of introductions and joking and applause, the speaker signaled and the drumming resumed. The line of people waiting between the drums began its slow procession.

The entry was headed by several Native American princesses and a color guard of military veterans. Behind the flags, the line of people was four across and appeared endless in length. Most of the dancers were wearing traditional dress and they danced with a series and pattern of movements as individual as the decorations on their clothing. Some high-stepped with arms raised, some kept feet low to the ground, some moved face forward, always tall and unbent, some turned and leaned in wide arcs.

The chain moved forward and began to circle around itself, snaking into a spiral. Cory supposed it all had meaning, some age-old significance, but of that she understood nothing, sensed nothing. Still, she thought that the stream of dancing color was perhaps the most stunning thing she had ever seen.

A flash of orange caught her eye, and she noticed a single dancing figure. She laughed, catching her mother's attention and earning a frown.

"Be polite," her mother said in a low voice.

"That boy," Cory said, pointing. "It looks like he couldn't wait to join the party."

The dancer who attracted her attention was twirling and dipping at the edge of the chain. His arms were raised as if to take hold of some personal music, and he danced as if the drum played for him alone. No feathers, no fringe, no traditional dress at all. The boy wore a marine corps T-shirt, orange Zubaz pants, and sneakers. Every now and then his arm would drop from its dance position and he would push up his glasses.

"It's all quite a spectacle," Margaret said.

Cory nodded as she watched the orange Zubaz dance away. "It's wonderful."

Roxanne's arm shot out and she pointed to an indeterminate spot across the dance floor. She turned to a friend behind her. "Look at Harvey MacNamara. He's obviously adjusting to small-town life."

"Yes," answered the friend. "Living with Barb must be good for him."

Roxanne leaned to Cory's mother and whispered something in her ear. "You're right," Margaret said. "He is nice-looking."

Cory tracked their collective gaze and settled on a

handsome, middle-aged man standing behind the host drum. The older women were laughing, and Cory rolled her eyes. It always amused her and sometimes embarrassed her when her mother's friends too obviously enjoyed scoping out men. Acting as if they were, well, Cory's age.

The dance area was packed, and the people were now just moving in place. Orange Zubaz had disappeared, and Cory lost interest in the dance. She turned to the women's conversation.

"Harvey," Roxanne was explaining to those around her, "moved into Barb's two weeks ago. Her kids just love him. He was living with his brother, but Tom checked into rehab. It's tough on Harvey, of course. He's been almost mother and father to Tom for years now."

Cory rose and stretched. Adult gossip was no fun. She whispered to her mother, "I'm going to walk around."

"Don't be gone too long. I'm beat, and I might not make it much longer."

"We could go now."

"Take a look around, then come back."

Cory squeezed her mother's shoulder and slipped into the crowd.

Tables of crafts were set up around the perimeter of the room. Cory moved from table to table, admiring the items but finding nothing of particular interest until she came to a jewelry display. She stopped when she spotted a pair of silver earrings designed in an intricate, webbed pattern. Cory smiled at the table attendant, picked up the earrings, and laid them on her palm. She turned over the price tag and tried not to gasp. Fifty-five dollars. She returned them to the table.

"Prices might go down Sunday afternoon," a voice next to her whispered.

She turned and looked into the chest and then the brown eyes of Orange Zubaz.

"A few of the vendors jack them up on Saturday nights because of the white tourists from the ski areas who come to watch the powwow."

"I'm not a tourist."

"I know that. You're Cory Knutson. We go to the same school."

"We do?" She studied his face and felt certain she had never seen him before tonight. "I'm sorry, I just don't recognize you."

Other people edged them aside, and Orange Zubaz tugged on Cory's sleeve. "Over here." They stepped away from the table and sat down on chairs pushed up against the wall.

He waved to someone in the crowd, then turned to Cory. She wondered if he ever stopped smiling.

"Don't apologize. I'm a senior and I just moved to Summer from Milwaukee. I'm a stranger, but apparently everyone knows Cory K." He offered his hand. "Harvey MacNamara."

"Harvey MacNamara?" she said, her voice squealing up an octave.

His smile disappeared and his hand dropped. "Yeah, Harvey MacNamara."

Cory knew she needed to explain her surprise.

22

"Your name," she began, then laughed a bit as she recalled the women's conversation.

"What's wrong with it — not Indian enough? Maybe you think it should be something cute, like Fast as a Dead Coyote?"

She looked at him evenly. "No. My mother's friend was talking about this guy Harvey MacNamara who is living with her sister. I thought he'd be older."

His good humor returned, and she relaxed. He wasn't gorgeous or anything, but he certainly did have a make-you-melt smile.

"You must mean Roxanne. She talks a lot, but she's one good person. And I'm not 'living with' Barb, okay? I'm just there. After all, she has a husband."

"I don't really know the family."

"Barb is sort of a cousin of my mother's, and I needed a place to live." He clasped his hands together, and the action caused the muscles visible under the T-shirt to flex. Cory looked away; she now knew the meaning of the word *biceps*. She exhaled deeply and wondered how the room had suddenly filled with hot August air.

"Are you okay?" he asked.

"I'm fine."

"You look a little woozy. Would you let me buy you something to eat and drink?"

"Food would be nice. I haven't eaten since noon. But, Harvey, you don't have to buy."

"Please call me Mac. Harvey's an old guy's name, right? I'd like to buy because you're a guest here. Anyway, aren't you supposed to be broke because you're

23

paying off that window? I heard it was a pretty good smashup."

Cory groaned. "Everyone. Everyone."

He guided her through the crowd to the food stands, and just as they stepped up to place their orders for wild rice with mushroom sauce, Cory felt a tug on her shirt. She turned and saw Roxanne.

"Found you!" Roxanne said. She nodded to Mac.

"What's up?"

"Your mother wants to go." She held out Cory's coat. "She was exhausted and the heat and stuffy air made it worse. She's waiting outside the main door. I'll go home with Paula. Margaret's not well, Cory. I'm sorry I urged her to come."

"She really wanted to, Roxanne. Mac, I'm sorry."

"Another time. Glad we met."

Roxanne watched them smile at each other. "Well, Harvey." She laughed.

He frowned. "Mac, it's Mac."

She shrugged and turned to Cory. "Don't keep her waiting. I'm sure *Mac* would love to show you out."

He walked Cory outside to where her mother was waiting, and Cory introduced them.

"See you in school," he said as they separated.

"Monday. Hey, Mac," she said, pausing to let her mother get a few steps away. "I really liked your dancing."

He was pleased. "You saw?"

"I was watching."

He smiled, saluted, then turned with a step and a

dip. She laughed and watched as the boy in orange Zubaz danced into the building.

"Roxanne says he's been in and out of six schools in six years while his brother moved them around, but he's always kept up a good average. B's, at least," Cory's mother said, leaning her head against the seat of the car and closing her eyes.

Snow was falling, obscuring the white lines of the deserted highway. Trying to keep the car centered in the proper lane, Cory focused on a distant, imaginary spot in the road. It would be a slow thirty miles home.

"She also said other good things. He —"

"Mom, I don't need to hear the secondhand details of his life, okay? We just met, that's all."

"Is it? Sometimes mothers can see these things with a different perspective."

"Right: warped."

"Change of subject, then. Did you enjoy the pow-wow? I mean, for reasons other than the obvious one." She laughed, believing she had said something funny.

Cory reached to punch her playfully, but her mother raised a hand. "Watch your driving, girl."

The snow was falling faster and attacking the windshield like silent white bullets. Cory switched the wipers to high. "I did enjoy it. The clothing was fantastic."

"I'm sorry we had to leave early and miss the actual dance competition."

"Another time."

"What I loved seeing was the young and old together. All those mothers and daughters in matching fancy dresses. Roxanne plans to make her own jingle dress so she can dance with Paula."

"Don't get any ideas about us. Maybe like doubling at my prom."

"I know better." She folded her arms and laid them across her chest. "But what do we do together, Cory? What have I passed on to you?"

An oncoming car with high beams approached. Cory flicked her lights to signal the other driver to lower his. "You must be tired, Mom. You sound so melancholy."

"It's important to pass things on. What have I taught you?"

"To be nice to people and to wear beige bras under white shirts."

"That's all?"

"They're both important lessons, especially the bra thing. I hate showing underwear lines through clothing."

Margaret laughed and sat erect. She looked out the side window, finding something of interest beyond the curtain of falling snow. "Let's go canoeing this summer. I used to do that when I was your age. We'll go to Canada for a week, just the two of us."

Cory wrinkled her brow. She hated canoe camping but didn't want to press the issue now. "Sure, Mom."

Her mother eased back down into a comfortable position and soon fell asleep. Cory sang to herself and stared into the white abyss beyond the windshield. After a few mesmerizing minutes she thought she saw the shapes of dancers in colorful attire amidst the snow-flakes. Once or twice she even saw the flash of orange. She blinked away the mirage, gripped the wheel, and willed herself to stay alert. Though she now saw only the swirling snow, nothing she could do or hum would shake loose the haunting sound of the drum. It sang to her all the way home.

3

CORY LOOKED for Mac at school on Monday. She asked everyone she knew about him, but none of her friends could tell her anything about a senior transfer from Milwaukee. By lunchtime she had almost convinced herself that meeting him had been simply the nicest of dreams. While sitting in the cafeteria with the usual crowd, she even contemplated crossing over to the next table to ask those students about Mac.

"Cory, cut it out," Karin said. "You've been staring at the Reservation for fifteen minutes now. What's up?"

"Don't call it that, Karin."

Karin stole one of Cory's chips. "We always have. But, okay, how about 'Indian Territory'?" She giggled at her wit.

"Racist, Karin. Don't be racist."

Karin grew serious. "Are you turning into one of those liberals who screams 'racist!' every time someone tries to breathe?"

28

"I'm with Cory," said Sasha. "Any sort of name-calling is offensive."

Karin ignored Sasha. "Does this new sensitivity have anything to do with a senior transfer from Milwaukee? The one you have been hunting down all morning?"

Cory picked up Karin's sandwich. "Put that in your mouth and chew." Karin took it and made a face. Cory stuffed the remains of her lunch into its paper bag, wadded that, then aimed and tossed it at the trash barrel near the end of their table. The bag hit the rim of the barrel and fell in.

"Two points," said Tony.

"The team could have used you Saturday night," said Sasha. "It was sad."

"A thirty-point loss," said Karin. "Nick and I left early because we just couldn't watch anymore. Thirty points, to Forest Lake! I was embarrassed to be wearing a Summer sweatshirt."

"And I bet you let Nick take it off as soon as you were in the car," said Tony.

"What a whiner," Cory said, ignoring Tony. "It was their first loss all season."

"It was pathetic," Karin said emphatically. She pointed across the lunchroom. "I'm surprised they even want to show their faces here."

Cory considered stuffing something in Karin's face but found nothing suitable. She shrugged and looked to where Karin had pointed.

The population of the cafeteria hushed as four members of the girls' basketball team hesitantly stood and scanned the room for a place to sit. The atmosphere was barbed with the school's nearly universal reproach and disappointment.

"Thirty points," Karin said. "Embarrassing."

"*You* are embarrassing," Cory said. Suddenly she raised her arms, then pounded down on the table with her fists. "Yea, Stormers!" she bellowed. She pounded again. "Yea, Stormers!" Pound. "Yea, Stormers!" Pound. Tony and Sasha joined her, then another table, and another. By the time Cory's hands were red and stinging from the pounding, the cheer had grown to a tumultuous and deafening uproar.

It wasn't enough. Cory stood on the table and urged on the cheering by clapping her hands over her head and swaying back and forth. The demonstration finally subsided when she jumped off the table to hug the team captains, who had made their way through the crowd to Cory's table.

Cory picked up her book bag and smiled at Karin. "That was fun, but it's time for algebra."

Mac was sitting alone at a table near the front of the cafeteria. He was eating and reading. Cory spotted him as she followed her friends out of the room. She walked over to him.

He looked up and smiled. "Hey, hey, it's Cory K."

"You really do go to school here. I was beginning to wonder." She sat down across from him and needed a moment to catch her breath. Either she was limp and drained from the cheering, or his smile was working its magic again. He leaned forward. His glasses had slipped down his nose a bit. Cory restrained the impulse to reach out and gently push them up.

"Cory . . ."

"Yeah?"

"I liked your dancing."

She shook her head. "Not exactly dancing. When I dance I *move*. Like you, Mac."

He held his sandwich between his fingertips and stared at it.

"Must be a pretty interesting sandwich," she said. "Peanut butter?"

He looked up. "Salami. Cory . . ." He stared again at his sandwich.

Though she'd never had a steady boyfriend, Cory had been dating since ninth grade and she quickly recognized the signs of a boy's interest. She saw them now in Mac and immediately engaged herself in a speedy mental debate. Did she want to? Yes, she realized, she did.

Mac looked up, looked around, looked again at his sandwich. Obviously, she was going to have to help him. "Mac, maybe you could —"

"Cory, you're wanted in the office. Now."

Cory turned and saw Mrs. Hartwig, the lunchroom supervisor and possessor of the world's largest voice. She faced Mac again.

Mrs. Hartwig laid a hand on her shoulder. "Now, Cory."

Mac smiled. "I guess they just got word of the riot up in the office."

"I suppose I'll get one of Mr. Donaldson's famous lectures." She tried to shrug off the woman's hand, but it wouldn't slip loose.

"Upstairs, Cory," the woman said.

31

"What were you going to say?" asked Mac. "Maybe I could what?"

The woman's claw pressed on Cory's shoulder. "Call me?" asked Cory.

Mac tapped her on the hand. "You'd better go; she's about to lose it. I'll call you later."

Cory rose and grabbed her bag. "It's listed under Mike Knutson, Big Bass Road." She turned and followed Mrs. Hartwig out of the cafeteria, and they walked across the crowded room accompanied by a wave of applause. Cory bowed to the cheers.

"It wasn't really a riot," Cory said to the principal as soon as she was in his office. "You know I wouldn't do that, Mr. Donaldson."

He waved his hand to silence her. "Your father is on his way —"

"That's ridiculous! All I —"

"Your mother collapsed at work, Cory. Doc Scudder took a look and sent her by ambulance to the regional hospital in Wausau. Mike is on his way to get you so that the two of you can drive down together. They had to resuscitate her. I hate to tell you this, Cory, but they said it doesn't look good."

"I don't know a damn thing more," Mike said as Cory got into the car. "Not a damn thing." It was the last either of them spoke until they had driven at racecar speed the sixty miles to Wausau.

The hospital was at the edge of town. Mike parked in the emergency lot and rested his head against the steering wheel. "Oh, God, please," he said then.

Cory held back as they approached the emergency desk. If her mother was dead, she would know by watching Mike. She couldn't bear to hear it from a nurse while standing in a room full of strangers. Mike spoke to someone behind the desk and didn't collapse, so Cory stepped to his side.

". . . stabilized first, then monitored carefully. Can't say what caused it. Tests during the next few days will determine that." The nurse looked at Cory. "No, you can't see her right now."

Cory didn't know she had even asked the question. Ninety minutes earlier she had been dancing on a tabletop; now she moved and thought and spoke in a fog of shock and fear.

The fog lifted slightly two hours later when she was allowed to see her mother. Sleeping or unconscious, pale and still, her mother lay among the wires and tubes.

"Oh, Mom," Cory whispered. Then she kneeled and laid her cheek against her mother's hand.

4

HEART TROUBLE had never meant more to Cory than the problems her friends had when they were ignored or dumped by their boyfriends. Within a few days of her mother's hospitalization, however, she learned a broader definition. She now knew about the three layers of heart tissue. She knew about the Greek roots of the word *cardiomyopathy*. She knew that diseased and weakened heart muscles could go undetected for too long while they grew large, thick, stiff, and incompetent. She knew that complete rest and medications could maintain a diseased heart temporarily. She knew that without a transplant her mother would die.

"I want some salt," Margaret Knutson said to her daughter. "It's the strongest craving I've ever had, worse than wanting sex. Cory, you didn't really hear that."

"I did, but I'd rather not talk about it."

"I can't believe I will never again eat a pile of fries loaded with fat and salt."

"You never did before and you certainly never will now. Should I pack these hospital slippers?"

"Gorgeous, aren't they? Almost as gorgeous as I feel. Pack them. Take everything. We can throw it out when we get home."

A nurse entered the room pushing a wheelchair. "Let's load you up and get you out. They're predicting another five inches of snow by night and you don't want to drive through that."

Cory couldn't wait to leave the hospital. She couldn't wait to get away from the mauves and grays, the indiscernible intercom voices, the cafeteria food and vending-machine coffee. It had been a terrible ten days, but at last she and Mike were taking her mother home.

They had spent that first awful night in the hospital lounge. At midnight Rob had arrived, bursting into the lounge with pent-up anguish and uncertainty. Cory had watched as Mike soothed his stepson and explained what little they knew. Rob was strung tight and spent most of the night switching chairs, rebinding his ponytail, and buying fresh cups of coffee. His restlessness was comforting to Cory, as it was something she had known in him forever. Hurricane Rob, everyone had called him. Rob had raced to grow up, her mother said: walking at nine months, swimming at two, building forts and rafts before he was in school, first gun at eight, first deer at ten, and, he'd recently confessed to Cory, first sex at fourteen.

Once she knew her brother was there and worrying, Cory could sleep. And she took the first of many lousy naps curled uncomfortably into a stiff-backed, scratchy waiting-room chair.

The second night they rented a motel room, but no one wanted to sleep there. Then the next day, reassured that Margaret was no longer in imminent danger, Rob returned home. Later that afternoon, after exchanging a few words with her groggy mother, Cory went home, too, full driving privileges restored. She quit her job, collected missed schoolwork, and called a long list of concerned friends. Then, every day for another week, she drove from Summer to the hospital after school, bringing Mike fresh clothes and delivering cards and letters to her mother.

It was a rough week. She failed two tests, skipped another, lost some favorite earrings, had a flat on the highway, and gained five pounds.

Sitting and eating, sitting and eating. That was it. So, as the nurse pushed the wheelchair out of the hospital to where Mike was waiting with the truck, Cory felt like jumping on a table and dancing.

Instead, she pounded on the engine hood. "Take us home!" she cheered.

Two miles out of town, Margaret turned on the radio and started singing along. "You can't imagine how good it feels to be going home. You can't." She resumed singing loudly.

"I know where I get my voice from," said Cory. "I love you, Mom, but this isn't pleasant."

"Don't sing," said Mike. "Don't sing, don't dance, don't whistle, don't work, don't carry firewood, don't eat salt."

"Don't have sex," whispered Cory.

"I didn't hear that," said her mother. She turned to her husband. "Did they tell us that?"

"Don't do anything until they find the right heart and put it in," Mike said.

"It will be a good chance for me to catch up on the soaps."

"You've never watched the soaps, Margaret. You've worked your whole life. That stops now."

"Being an invalid might not be half bad. I can just lie around and watch the two of you do everything."

"A plot," said Cory. "This was all a plot to get out of doing your share."

Her mother closed her eyes and smiled. "A bit extreme, but that's what it took." A new song began on the radio. "Turn it up, Cory. That's Crosby, Stills, and Nash. 'Suite: Judy Blue Eyes.' The best song ever."

Cory turned up the dial. "These guys are old men. I saw them on television last month."

"They weren't when they did this song. Listen to those guitars. Oh, how I wish I had gone to Woodstock."

Mike's laughing drowned out the music for nearly half a mile. "Margaret," he said finally, "it's not your heart that's sick, it's your brain. I can understand how a brush with death would make you think back and do some wishing, but Woodstock? You wish you had spent three days going naked in the rain and mud?"

"The music, darling. I wish I had been there for the music." She turned to Cory. "Be sure you marry a man who doesn't laugh at you."

"In 1969," Mike said, "you were twenty-two, married, a mother, and still active in the church. Lord, Woodstock."

The roads were snow-covered and slippery, and Mike drove slowly. But as they headed home together, their spirits soared, and they could have been flying. They marveled at the beauty of the familiar scenery, Mike told his best stories, and Margaret taught them to sing the "doo-doo-doo" part of The Best Song Ever. The hospital was behind them, and they hadn't yet reached home, where they would live with the fearful uncertainty of Cory's mother's precarious health. For a treasured two hours, Cory sat between her two favorite people, talked, listened, and sang. She had never been so happy.

5

"AREN'T HEART transplants expensive, like thousands?" Cory asked Mike. She glanced at the rollaway bed on the other side of the living room where her mother was sleeping, and would always sleep until a new heart was found, transplanted, and healed. They had been told that climbing stairs was as dangerous as eating salt, or running, or working. Everyone was adjusting.

"These days a tetanus booster costs thousands. But yes, it is expensive. Bless the union, though; it's almost all covered."

Cory closed her math book. The twenty remaining problems could wait, maybe forever. "Almost covered?"

"The medical part will be taken care of, but there are plenty of other things that won't be: our expenses for staying in Minneapolis while she's hospitalized at the transplant unit; equipment rental, like that bed;

some of the prescriptions; and a home health aide for after surgery."

"I'll take care of her, Mike. We won't need anyone. It's why I quit my job, so I could be around. And now that you've canceled my debt, I feel like I should be doing more."

"You'll be doing plenty, Cory. She and I were talking about that this afternoon, and we don't want you to be enslaved by her illness. We aren't going to let that happen."

"She's my mother. It's not slavery."

"Listen to you! Just two weeks ago when we would try to get you to finish a chore list around here, all we heard was moaning about child labor laws."

"Helping now is different. Mom wasn't dying then."

Dying. It was the first time either of them had said the word. And when they heard it — as if it came not from Cory's lips but somewhere else, a surprise — its effect was not to increase their already immeasurable sadness, but to lay down a bridge between them. They shared the nightmare.

Cory rifled the pages of a notebook, and a paper slipped out. A large D was visible for a moment before she turned the paper over. "Mike, things haven't been great at school lately. Maybe it would make sense for me to drop out until after the surgery. I could be around to help."

"That is the most ridiculous thing I've heard yet. Do you think it would help her to have you drop out of school?"

"But what about those expenses? Can we do it?"

40

Mike had disappeared into himself. He was usually affectionate and outgoing, the first person in the house to notice another's unhappiness. But since his wife's illness had taken over family life, he had begun to withdraw quietly. Cory would see him standing at a window or sitting hand in hand with her mother, and she could tell he was off on some silent, personal journey.

He had withdrawn now, and Cory gently nudged him back. "Mike," she said a bit louder, "all that money — do we have it? Can we do it?"

He looked at her as if the question made no sense. "Of course, Cory. We'll do it."

The town would do it. Within three days of Margaret Knutson's return home, a community-sponsored fund in her name was opened at the bank, and a committee to plan and coordinate fund-raising events was formed.

Within ten days, a rummage sale and craft fair were held. Timed to coincide with an influx of visitors to a winter sports festival at a nearby resort, they raised six hundred dollars. Change buckets were placed by every cash register in town, and a series of community events — pancake breakfast, spaghetti supper, covered-basket auction, and dance — was scheduled.

"The next time I need a new heart," Margaret said to Cory and Roxanne, "I will arrange to have it happen in the summer. Look at that snow coming down. Only fools would drive through this to eat spaghetti."

"Fools," said Roxanne, "or people who love Margaret Knutson. Good grief, woman, is that husband of yours always so slow getting ready?"

"Always."

"It's one of the reasons they quit going to church," said Cory. "They could never get there on time." She sat on one of the several chairs that had been arranged around her mother's bed. Roxanne was sitting in for the evening to keep Margaret company while Mike and Cory went to the fund-raiser. She was one of many friends who had organized a loose system of support so Mike and Cory could have time off from the intense caretaking. But even when a good friend was there to keep her mother company, Cory hated leaving. It was usually fun to hang around and listen while her mother joked or reminisced with friends. But because tonight's dinner was a fund-raiser for the family, she and Mike felt obligated to go.

"How do I look?" Mike stood behind them, tucking in the tail of his shirt.

Roxanne and Cory whistled, and Margaret shook her head. "A tie? Since when a tie?"

He walked over and kissed her. "The husband of the invalid should look his best. Let's go, Cory. You're holding us up." He wagged a finger at his wife and then looked sternly at Roxanne. "Be good, both of you."

"We'll have a great time," Roxanne said. "After we watch *Alien,* we plan to call some nine-hundred numbers and talk to young men."

Cory and her mother laughed while Mike chewed on his lip. "Aren't you a grandmother?" he asked.

"Three times over," Roxanne said. "Now get out of here."

"I know the phone-calling is a joke, but you aren't really going to watch *Alien,* are you? It's pretty scary. She almost didn't make it through the first time she saw it and she had a good heart then."

"Mike, please go," said Margaret. "I'm not going to do anything more exciting than get up and shuffle to the bathroom."

Roxanne followed them to the door and waited with Cory while Mike went ahead to warm up the car. "You be nice to Mac. He volunteered to help in the kitchen tonight."

"I'm always nice to him."

"Too bad things didn't work out differently."

"There was nothing to work out, Roxanne. I explained to him that I just don't feel like dating these days."

"I know, but Barb said she could tell he was disappointed. I think it would be good —"

Cory pressed her finger against Roxanne's lips and shushed her. "I sure can tell that you're somebody's mother because the advice just flows out of you." The car horn honked, and Cory zipped up her jacket. "Take it easy, Mom," she called. "And it's okay about Mac," she said to Roxanne. "He knows what's going on. He understands."

Mac did understand. During the first week after the family's return from Wausau, he had called twice and a few times approached Cory at school, sometimes shyly working his way to her side when she was with

43

friends, but more often finding her when she was alone at her locker.

She appreciated his concern and kindness and was always glad to see him, but the strong interest and attraction she had felt during their first conversations had subsided. Her mother was sick and possibly dying. Dealing with a boyfriend, making time for dates, and waiting for phone calls all seemed like meaningless distractions.

"Not now, Mac," she'd explained when he at last asked her to a movie. "Dating just isn't where I'm at these days." And he had said he understood.

The friendship attracted some attention. There were no interracial couples in school and even few interracial conversations. So when Mac sat at her lunch table or walked her from school to her car, Cory could almost count on receiving phone calls that evening from friends.

The calls irritated her, and she had even hung up on Karin, who had said that she would never under any circumstances kiss an Indian. Logan Bennett, a senior who had never done more than nod to Cory at council meetings, called twice to ask her out. When she turned him down the second time, he'd responded curtly, "You like Indians better?"

"Better than you," she'd answered.

"I hope the spaghetti tastes better than the pancakes," Mike said as they entered the senior citizens' center.

"A pig roast," said Cory. "That would be a delicious charity. Do the beggars dare make suggestions?"

"I don't think so. Look at this crowd." Mike waved to someone and, at the same time, hundreds of eyes turned on them.

Cory was accustomed to being well known in a small town, but now she was almost a celebrity and she didn't like it. She felt as if she were constantly being watched, discussed, and evaluated: She's holding up so well. She's such a help. She's slipping in school. Do you suppose she ever cries?

As she felt the eyes watching, she wished she had stayed home. That was a difference the family situation made. Before, she never passed up social gatherings and often turned them into her own party. In a way, these fund-raising events were for her, but they never *ever* felt like a party.

Mike forged into the crowd — shaking hands, accepting hugs, joking and laughing. Cory held back; she doubted she could fake it tonight.

"I will be personally offended if you sneak away without eating anything."

Cory turned. "Hi, Mac. Look at you — what a mess!" He was wearing a long white apron that was soaked and splattered with kitchen juices and food bits.

"Chef Mac, please."

"I didn't know you cooked."

"And you probably didn't know that spaghetti is a traditional Native American dish."

She sniffed. "Smells like you were on garlic duty."

"And onions. I chopped about fifteen pounds. That was all they trusted me to do. Actually, I can't even cook a scrambled egg without ruining it. I always get shell mixed in."

"Did I really look like I wanted to sneak away?"

He was holding a plastic cup. He sipped before answering. "You did. Don't go." He pointed across the room. "Sasha and Tony are sitting with Barb's kids at the table by the podium. Go sit with them. They're safe."

"Safe?"

"It just doesn't look like you are up to forcing cheerfulness tonight."

"Can you read minds?"

"Another Native specialty. Pretty scary, huh?"

"It is. Oh well, I don't think I can avoid it any longer. If Mike can do it, so can I."

"You sit with Sasha and Tony, and I'll bring the food and join you."

Cory nodded. "Sounds good. But I'll need ten minutes to get there through this crowd. Wish me luck."

It took twenty. People she had known her entire life and people she barely knew wanted to talk, or hug, or introduce Cory to a guest. She smiled and laughed, returned the embraces, and thanked everyone for coming. She was grateful for the support, but it was exhausting.

Mac arrived at the table just as she did. "I could tell you wouldn't get here that soon," he said as he set a plate in front of her. He nodded greetings to Tony and Sasha, and spoke to the three children. "Behaving?"

"They've been great," said Sasha. "Tell their mother

I'll baby-sit anytime." She turned to the three girls seated opposite her at the table. "Sing Mac the song I taught you."

"Please don't," said Tony. "Sorry, kids," he said to the girls, "but I've already heard it fifteen times."

The middle girl was undeterred. She placed her hands on her hips, sashayed a few times in her seat, then started singing. "My name is Aphrodite, I'm the goddess of love. I get my sexy attributes from Zeus up above. I've got the sex appeal —"

Mac stopped her with a raised hand. "Jessa, how old are you?"

"Eight."

Cory was laughing so hard she spilled food on her shirt. "Darn. Wouldn't you know I'd wear white?"

"Do you want to hear the rest of the song?" Jessa asked.

"Why don't you ask Cory about last Halloween —" Sasha interjected.

"Please, Sasha, don't."

"When she sang that song —"

"Stop it, Sash."

"To the high school principal."

The little girls squealed disbelief, and Mac stopped eating, his fork frozen in midair. "Really?" he asked.

Tony nodded. "It was great. For the Halloween dance last year, Cory dressed up as this incredible, sexy bombshell. You couldn't recognize her."

"That's not a compliment," Cory said.

"But it's true," Sasha said. "She wore a red wig, four-inch heels, and loads of makeup."

"She stuffed her chest," said Tony. "Really stuffed. What a difference!"

Cory tossed a wadded napkin at him and, for as long as she could resist, didn't look at Mac, not wanting to see where he was looking. When she finally peeked, he was smiling right at her.

"Everyone was fooled," Sasha said. "Donaldson was in the gym chaperoning the dance, and she goes up to him and sings."

"What did he do?" Mac asked.

"Nothing," said Cory. "He just looked tired. I think the guy's been a principal too long. Nothing bothers him."

"So, you see," Sasha said to the girls, "I learned that song from Cory K., and now I have taught it to you."

The girls stood up and started bumping hips and singing. Mac finally succeeded in quieting them and they resumed eating. He turned to Sasha. "Thanks for watching the kids."

"No problem."

"But," he paused and seemed to be weighing his words, "a song about sexiness and Greek gods isn't really appropriate for American Indian kids. I don't know how their parents will feel about it."

Sasha paled in distress. "Mac, I had no idea."

Cory looked at Mac. His face was still and serious, but she discerned something agitating. "Sasha, I think he's pulling your chain." Mac's face relaxed into a smile.

Tony burst out laughing. "Oh, man, he's got you figured out."

"I'm sorry, Sasha," said Mac. "I was teasing. The song is fine. I even bet that in a few days they'll probably have Barb singing it to them at bedtime."

"She'll like it," agreed Jessa. "She's always singing songs."

"Your problem," Tony said to Sasha, "is that you get your rules out of some 'How To Be a Liberal' manual. You worry too much about doing the wrong thing."

"Too much?" she snapped. "That's impossible. And maybe you should worry more."

"Look what you've done," Cory said to Mac. "They're going to fight."

Sasha was clenching her fork and staring at Tony. Mac tugged on her sleeve. "Get mad at me," he said. "I'm the one who was teasing."

"But he's the one who enjoyed seeing me get caught. The jerk."

Tony sat back and stared daggers at Sasha. She turned away from him.

Cory leaned over the table and clasped her hands together. "Please, not in front of the children." Mac and the girls laughed, and the warring couple softened visibly.

Mac tapped Sasha on the back of her hand. "You owe me."

"For what?"

"He'll feel guilty and be nice to you for at least a day now."

Tony touched Sasha's neck and lightly massaged. "I'm sorry."

"He's such a wimp," Cory said to Jessa and her sisters, who were watching the scene with wide-eyed rapture. "He should wait and make her work for the apology."

"Let's pretend all this never happened," said Sasha.

"Good idea," said Mac. "And I don't believe anyone can care too much about doing wrong things. Or right things. Which would it be?"

"Depends where you are," Sasha said. "In this sad town people need to worry about *why* they do the wrong things."

"Don't say that," said Cory. "You've only lived here a year. And after what people have done for my mother, no one can criticize. There are plenty of good souls in Summer."

"Maybe so, but they all live separately. Look around. This is the first integrated event I've seen since I moved here."

"That's just how things are," said Tony. "We've talked about it a hundred times. It doesn't make us bigots."

"Everything's segregated."

"By choice. And it's mutual."

"Everything except the movie theater and the Dairy Queen. Even the bars are segregated, right?"

"Especially the bars," said Mac. "I've seen that in every town I've lived in."

Sasha turned to Cory. "But not this dinner. You should be proud about that."

Cory twisted the last strands of pasta around her plastic fork. "I get what you're saying, Sash, but I don't really want to view my mother's illness as a social victory for a racist town."

"It's a moral victory."

"Watch out," said Tony. "When she starts talking about morality it means she's shifted into high gear. And then there's no stopping her." He looked at the little girls. "Maybe you should sing that song again. I bet Cory would climb up on the table and dance along." The girls cheered and looked pleadingly at Cory.

"No," she said. "Simply no."

Before they could begin begging, their mother appeared at the table. "We've had some complaints about the noise level over here," she said with false sternness. "What's going on?"

"Sasha taught us a song," said Jessa. "Do you want to hear it?"

"Save it for bedtime," said her mother. "Which is coming up very soon." Her daughters protested, but she silenced them with an upraised palm. "Tony and Sasha, it was nice to meet you, and thank you for sitting with the girls while I was in the kitchen. I hope you didn't mind that Mac volunteered you." She turned to him. "I just got a call from Jeff. He says Willy is feeling worse and wants me home."

Willy was Barb and Jeff's twelve-year-old son. Barb had dropped off Roxanne at Cory's house earlier that evening before driving to Dumont's Meat Locker in Millersburg to pick up the eighty pounds of donated meatballs. She had mentioned then that her son wasn't well.

51

"Does he still have his fever?" Cory asked.

"Yes, and my husband says it's higher. Mac, the girls and I will walk home. It's only three blocks. If I leave you the keys, would you drive out and get Roxanne? I'd send Jeff, but he's due at work in an hour."

He nodded. "Of course."

"Girls, thank Tony and Sasha and clear your plates." They rose obediently, said their thank-yous and good-byes, and cleared their tableware into a large trash bin. They ran toward an exit and disappeared.

Barb drummed her fingers on Mac's shoulder. "Maybe you can give Cory a ride home."

"Maybe I can."

"Good night, kids," Barb said.

"Time for us to go, too," said Sasha briskly. "Come along, Antonio. We have more making up to do."

Tony rose and stacked the empty dishes. "I love this part," he said. "It's why I pick so many fights."

Sasha hugged Cory. "Be good, you two."

Left alone, Mac and Cory said nothing until she spilled her water. Mac wiped it up with a handful of used napkins, and said, "I'd like to drive you home. I'm going that way."

"To get Roxanne. I heard. Mac, why am I so suspicious about all this?"

"About what?"

"Willy's illness, Roxanne being stranded at our place, Barb asking you to go get her. Was it some sort of matchmaker's plan?"

He dropped the sodden clump of napkins. "Roxanne's car is in the shop, Jeff has to go to work, and Willy is definitely sick. There's no conspiracy."

She watched his hands as he absently poked at the mound of napkins. Too often lately she'd caught herself staring at the Native American people she saw. She hated herself for doing it, but still she'd steal glances at the kids at school, or Roxanne or Peter when they came to the house, or the women in the stores. She realized that not long ago it was as if they were all invisible to her, people who were there but not seen. Now she couldn't help but look surreptitiously, fascinated with the faces, body types, and, especially, the varied palette of skin colors. Mac was not especially dark, but he was a deeper brown than she could ever hope to be, even if she spent a lifetime on a sunny island. She wanted to lay her hand next to his for the contrast, but instead curled it into a fist and set it on her lap.

"Are you still here?" he asked.

"I was wondering about . . ." Redskin. That certainly wasn't accurate. "Just wondering."

"About what? You were almost going to tell me."

"About why you always wear short sleeves in the winter."

"It's simple: I'm not a cold guy."

"I never thought you were." Mac suddenly chuckled. "What's the joke?" she asked.

"I was just picturing you dressed up and singing to the principal. Do you still have the outfit?"

"In my closet. You never know when you might need something slinky and sexy."

53

Mac raised his eyebrows. "I suppose not. Well, what's the verdict? May I take you home?"

Cory lifted her cup and eyed him over the rim. "What does it mean if I say yes?"

He shrugged. "Means I get a peek at something slinky and sexy."

She laughed in mid-sip. Water squirted out, coating her chin and shooting up her nostril. Mac handed her a dry napkin. "I can't refuse that deal," she said.

He leaned forward. "It's good to see you laugh."

"Even with water dripping out my nose?"

"Even then."

She wiped her face. "I realize I'm not much fun, Mac. Sorry."

"Don't apologize. Don't ever apologize, not for that."

"For something else?"

He pushed back from the table. "Maybe. You can apologize for not letting me take you home."

"You can take me home. Let's leave now."

"Aren't they going to have a program?"

"That's why I want to go now. I don't want to hear the president of the bank talk about my mother as if she were already dead."

He rose. "Let's go."

"I have to tell Mike, but I'm sure he won't mind."

Mike was the center of attention at a large table. Several people rose to offer Cory a seat, but she refused. She whispered her apologies and plans to Mike, who nodded and waved a greeting to Mac. Mike and Mac had never met, but Cory decided to postpone the introduction.

They walked quickly to the exit. She suspected her early departure would cause some comment, but in a small town like Summer even a trip to the gas station was a subject for conversation. It might appear that she was ungrateful for the community support, but tonight she just didn't care.

6

MAC TOOK some time to acquaint himself with the car's buttons and switches.

"You can drive, can't you?"

"Sure. Since I was twelve."

"But legally?"

"I have a license. I'm hesitating because usually I use their other car. It's older."

"It's cold, Mac. Let's get going."

"You people up here are obsessed with the weather, do you realize that? It dominates every conversation and it controls your activities."

"I get your point, and it's still cold."

He started the car and everything turned on: cold air burst out of the heat vents; the radio screamed; the wipers whooshed across the windshield. He adjusted the appropriate knobs, and the car calmed down.

Main Street was dark except for the green neon sign

over Thompson's Tap and the flashing beer logo over Paul's Pub.

"Segregated bars," said Mac. "Every town has them."

"Why did you move around so much?"

"My mother's life wasn't very settled. I even lived here in Summer once before."

"When?"

"For a few months when I was eight. That year my mom needed a place to stay and she came to Barb's. She made some new friends and had a good job, but she didn't want to stay through the winter. So we left. Another move. That's pretty much how it was, always moving around. Except we did spend two whole years in Oklahoma. After Mom died, I stayed with my brother, and he moved around, too."

Cory wanted to know everything. She wanted to ask and probe and hear about his life, which she knew must have been more complicated than anything she could imagine. They reached the edge of town, and Mac accelerated to highway speed. A mile went by before Cory mustered the nerve to begin the questions.

"How did your mother die?"

He tapped the steering wheel with his thumbs. "Car crash." He smiled at her. "I wasn't driving."

Cory tugged on her shoulder harness. "When?"

"Seven years ago. She was . . ." He reached and turned off the radio.

"Was what?" She could see that he was forming the story for telling. She waited.

He started over. "We were living in Nebraska when she died. She and my dad had split years earlier — he took off and disappeared when I was two — and, like I said, we moved around a lot. My brother is older, and he was gone already. For a short time we were in Missouri, and she had this boyfriend we were living with. Is this where I turn?"

"The next road, by the Big Bass Lake sign."

"Roger Trimble. He seemed okay, but then something changed or came up from down deep and he started slugging Mom around when he got mad. He did it twice, actually, and then we left. Mom didn't want to wait for it to happen again. She picked me up at school one day and we got out. But two months later he found us in Nebraska. We were living in Lincoln, and she was working at a bookstore. She always liked books. Maybe that's how he found her, by checking every bookstore in the Midwest. I was at school and never knew exactly what happened. But I figured out he must have tried to follow her home from work, and she tried to lose him. They both crashed on this gravel road outside of Lincoln. The cops figured they were going almost a hundred." He downshifted and turned onto the country road that led to Cory's home.

"I'm sorry, Mac. That's really terrible."

"At least *he* died, too. Otherwise I know I'd be after him, trying to track him down and beat the bastard to death."

"You feel like that?"

He was calm. "I feel like that."

He pulled into the driveway and parked the car next to the garage. The door was open, showing the empty space for Mike's truck. "My life hasn't been that great, but I've seen enough to learn a few things." He shifted in the seat, trying to find room to stretch his legs. "I've promised myself three things: I will always get good grades, I will never take a drink, and I will never hit a woman."

"Keep those promises and you can win a Boy Scout prize for virtue."

"It's not virtue."

"What is it?"

"Control. I just want to control what I can. So much else just spins away that I would feel helpless if I didn't believe I could control just those three things."

Cory looked at her hands and had the insane thought that it was time to redo her nails. Maybe pink.

"A lot of people romanticize being Indian these days," Mac continued. "The honest thing is that you always have this shadow right behind you. One wrong move in the white man's world, and bam! The good life disappears. Things are okay for me now — really pretty nice, everything considered. I'm working hard to keep them that way."

Cory curled her hands into fists. "I think you're right. Things do spin out of control. Sometimes the only thing I feel I can control" — she unfurled her fingers and wiggled them — "is my nail color."

He laughed. "I don't have that option. Cory, I don't want to be pushy, but if you've changed your mind about going out, I'd still like to."

Cory looked at the house. A single light over the deck cast distorted shadows around the yard.

"I understand something about what you're going through," he said. "During those years with my brother, he was sick a lot from his drinking. I know how hard it is to take care of someone, and how nice it would be to have a little personal attention."

Mac stared straight ahead when he spoke. She looked at him and recognized what she saw: a deep-set pain mixed with fear. Never apologize, he had said, and it was clear that with this guy there never would be a need for explanations or apologies for her unhappiness. Something inside turned around and opened. She could feel it.

He dropped his head a bit, and his glasses slid down. She reached out and pushed them up. He looked at her and smiled. "I'll take them off when I kiss you good night."

He did, and they did.

Once she had agreed to the change in their friendship, Cory fell hard and fell fast. She looked for Mac in the school hallways even when she knew he should be on the other side of the building, she watched the clock at night until he called, she savored their conversations for hours after they said good night. She was hooked.

"Why does one person ever like another?" She asked her mother as she gave her a shoulder rub. "Mac and I aren't magazine-pretty people, so it's not physical."

"Good. Keep it that way."

"So — why?"

"It's one of the eternal mysteries, Cory. Something just twists around inside, and you feel connected." She shifted and rolled onto her back. "That's good enough."

"More soup? You only had half a bowl."

"I'm fine. Don't clean up. Let's just sit and talk."

"I'll get the fire first." Small flames sputtered in the large fireplace on the wall opposite her mother's bed. Cory carefully added two more logs and adjusted them with her foot. One log tipped over and rolled onto the hearth, trailing sparks.

"Use the poker and tongs," her mother snapped.

Cory looked at her. "Feeling better tonight, aren't you?"

"I don't want to have to run out of a burning house."

Cory replaced the hot log. She picked up her tea mug and sat down next to the bed. They both stared at the renewed fire.

"Tell me about Mac."

"You've met him. He's been out here now maybe four times." She frowned. "Were you so groggy you don't remember?"

"Of course I remember. I just want to hear you describe the boy."

Cory held the mug up to her face, and the steam moistened her upper lip. She wiped it with her sweater cuff. "He's tall."

Her mother laughed. "He certainly is not tall, Cory.

61

Well, okay — maybe to you and me, but he's really no taller than five eight. For a man, that's not tall."

"Why don't you describe him, then?"

"I apologize. More, please."

"His hair is dark and thick and straight. He's letting it grow. He wears glasses. I think they need to be tightened."

"I remember the first time you saw him. The powwow."

Cory nodded. "The dancing orange Zubaz. He's built really solid, like Mike. You know how you always say Mike could get fat if he ever slowed down? I think Mac is like that. There's potential for a gut." She sipped and swallowed. "I don't think he shaves."

Her mother laughed. "Enough of the physical. Tell me about *him*."

Cory cradled her mug. "I've told you what I know about his family."

"About him."

"He can be funny, especially when he and Tony get going on something. They've gotten to be good friends."

"That's interesting. Jack Merrill is pretty proud about how much he hates Indians. Oh, the things I have heard that man say!"

"Like what?"

"Nothing that I want to repeat. Most of the time Jack can be so charming —"

"Charming? Tony's dad?"

"Very. And then an instant later he'll say the vilest

62

thing." She sat erect, raised her arms, and cupped her hands in a circle. "I've just wanted to wring his neck at times."

Cory put a hand on her mother's shoulder. "Settle down, Mom. Don't get so upset —"

Margaret patted her daughter's arm. "It's okay, dear. The thought of Jack's bigotry isn't going to kill me." She lay down. "I've often wondered where such feelings come from."

"Your murderous ones?"

"No. The bigotry. Where does it come from? Is it possible people are born with hate?"

"Do you want another shoulder rub?"

"I want an answer. Where does hate come from?"

"You're asking me?"

"I'm just asking. Anyone."

Pain was evident on her face. Cory didn't know if it came from the physical or the emotional anguish, from the uncertainty and discomfort of her health or from the perplexity posed by her world. Cory wished, a frequent wish, that she could wipe away all the trouble. Wished she could put her arms around her mother and fix it.

Margaret closed her eyes. "Hate must come from somewhere."

Cory stroked a few strands of hair off her mother's forehead. "School lunches."

Margaret opened her eyes and pushed up on an elbow. "What?"

"School lunches breed hate. What else could it be? Bigotry is everywhere in this country, right? And what's the common denominator? At one time or another everyone has eaten a school lunch. The big eaters are probably the big haters."

"Those mashed potatoes."

"The stuff they call meat."

Her mother was smiling now, and Cory's own heart lightened. For a moment, she'd fixed it.

"Jack Merrill must have always gone through the lunch line twice. Does Tony by any chance bring his own?"

Cory grinned. "He does."

"I'm glad he's different from his father."

"He wasn't always. He's sort of changed. He had to if he wanted to date Sasha."

"Good for her." She rolled onto her side and pulled the bedcover to her chin. "One heart at a time."

"What do you mean?"

"Would you tuck in the corner of the blanket? Mike calls it my theory of revolution."

"I didn't know you had one."

"Change a heart, you change the world. But doing it one heart at a time is the best you can hope for. Did you tuck it in?"

"Yes, Mom."

"I'm so cold. Could you get that striped blanket from the chair and spread it? Thanks. Much better. Mac is so polite to me and Mike. Is he nice to you?"

"Very nice. Not by holding doors, or doing that sort of thing. But he pays attention. I know he listens. Why are you laughing?"

"I'm not laughing at you, okay? I'm pleased. Any

64

healthy relationship is just a balancing act, Cory. Makes sense to me that you'd be happy with a quiet guy. A good balance."

"I didn't say he was quiet. I said he listens."

"My mistake. He strikes me as quiet."

Cory fixed her eyes on the fire. Not quiet, but still. Mac was still. And no matter what was going on with his life, he was a calm center for hers. Cory didn't want to burden her mother and complain. Didn't want to tell her how crazy things were, how the illness had blown into her life, picked her up by the heels, and started shaking. She couldn't tell her that in the middle of it all, Mac was a refuge. Things were still when they were together.

Margaret sat back on her pile of pillows. She breathed deeply several times, then closed her eyes. "Your first boyfriend."

"The first. Who was yours?"

"John Hanover. Lord, he was sweet."

"What happened?"

"Your father happened. He was sweeter. And he had a car."

Mike's voice charged through the back door seconds ahead of Mike. They turned to look as he walked toward them through the kitchen. Mac followed.

"Look who I found," Mike said. "Give me your coat, Mac, and go on in."

Mac pulled a small package out of his coat pocket before handing it over to Mike. "I got here fifteen minutes ago. I've been helping Mike put away the snowmobile."

"Only used the darn thing twice all winter," shouted Mike from the back entry where he'd gone to hang the wraps. He returned. "Might sell it next fall. Unless you'd miss it, Margaret."

"Not for a moment."

Mike rubbed his hands together and blew on them. "I need to warm up with some pie. Is there any left?"

"You've been outside twenty minutes, Mike," said Cory. "How could we eat a pie in twenty minutes?"

Margaret motioned Mac to sit down. "He made this heart-healthy pie today but couldn't decide if he wanted apple or cherry, so he put a crust down the middle and made half and half."

"The cherry looks better," said Mike. "Want some?"

Mac accepted, the other two declined.

"Good," said Mike as he walked toward the kitchen. "Mac and I will eat it all."

Mac handed the package he had brought to Margaret. "Barb has finally got her business going. I thought you might like one of the first pieces."

The delight and surprise Cory read in her mother's face mirrored her own. She couldn't imagine what nerve it must take for a boy to bring a gift to his girlfriend's mother.

Margaret untaped the package and smoothed back the tissue. A golden circle the size of a man's palm lay on the paper. Inside the circle, lines of gold crisscrossed in a webbed pattern similar to the earrings Cory had admired at the powwow. At the very center was an opening the size of a dime.

"An Ojibwa dream catcher," said Mac.

"Barb made this?"

He nodded. "She draws the pattern, then makes a stencil and uses that to cut it out of pressed metal."

"It looks like gold," said Cory.

"It is. Not exactly traditional material, but it sells better to the gift shops."

Margaret held it up by a short string laced through a small loop. The dream catcher spun around.

Mike returned with the pie. "Trying self-hypnosis?"

"He calls it a dream catcher. Explain that, Mac."

He took a plate from Mike and set it on his knee. "The tradition says if you hang it over your bed it will keep away the bad dreams and spirits. The bad ones are rough and get caught in the web, but the smooth, good ones slip through the little hole in the middle."

As she watched her mother trace the golden web with her finger, Cory suddenly felt like crying. Instead, she reached for Mike's pie plate. "Changed my mind," she said.

"Roxanne once told me," Margaret said to Mac, "that you're Cree."

"My father's people are, and most of my mother's. Some Ojibwa. My father is Métis Cree, technically. That's what the Canadians call mixed bloods. His grandfather was white."

"Canadian?" asked Cory.

"My parents were both born in Manitoba."

"She also said the Ojibwa and Cree were related," Margaret said. "Do the Cree have dream catchers?"

Mac finished his pie before answering. The others

waited. "I don't know. I wasn't raised with the traditions. I have no idea."

"Let's try it out," said Mike. He rose and removed a picture from the wall by the head of the bed. Margaret handed him the dream catcher and he slipped the string over the nail. It twisted slightly, changing colors as it captured and reflected the light from the fire.

"Tomorrow I'll screw in a plant hook," said Mike. "Then it can spin freely."

"Thank you, Mac," said Margaret. "I just love it."

"And it's time to let it work," said Mike. "You two kids can go talk in the basement, but it's lights-out for the patient."

"I have a physics test tomorrow," said Mac, "and I need to study more. I wanted to come out tonight because I'm going to Milwaukee after school to visit my brother."

Cory walked him to the back door where she retrieved his coat from the closet. "It's the middle of the week. Why go see him now?"

"He's checking out of the treatment center and wanted me along when he moves into the halfway house."

"Just a visit, right?"

He smiled. "I'm coming back."

"Thanks for her present. It was the sweetest thing," she whispered.

"Sweet?"

"Yes, sweet. Was it your idea or Barb's?"

He looked offended. "Totally mine. Although," he

said as he snapped up his coat, "Barb told me I could have it for less than cost."

Cory laid her head against his shoulder and closed her eyes. She did like saying good night to someone. Mom's absolutely wrong, she thought as he kissed the top of her head. Five eight *is* tall.

7

As Cory walked down the hallway with Mac and Tony, she looked ahead and saw a white triangle of paper sticking out of her locker. While the boys debated the merits of a movie they had rented the previous weekend, she pulled the paper out and unfolded it. The words slashed:

Only whores do it with injuns.

She swore softly, slapped her locker, and crumpled the paper.

"What's that?" asked Mac.

"A piece of junk." She dropped it in her bag and opened her locker. Mac fished in her bag and pulled out the paper. "Don't read it, Mac."

Tony looked over his shoulder. "Jerk," Tony finally muttered. Mac smiled.

"How can you laugh?" Cory demanded.

"I'm not laughing. It's just so . . . so wrong."

"Wrong?"

"Yeah. 'Only whores do it with injuns.' Well, you're not, you don't, and 'injuns' is pathetic name-calling. This guy should have asked me what word to use. I've heard some good ones."

"I don't like being called a whore."

"When I find the guy I'll beat him up."

"Very funny, Mac." She pulled two books from her locker and slammed it shut. She started to walk away. Mac grabbed her arm.

"Cory, I think the note is awful. But I've heard crap like that my whole life, and you can't let it get to you. Then they win."

"You should be angry."

"Who the hell says I'm not?" They froze as their words slammed into each other. People passing in the hall turned and looked at them.

Tony whistled. "You two sound like Sash and me. Must be love."

The warning bell rang and Cory and Mac resumed breathing. "See you at lunch?" she asked.

"No. I have to start an extra-credit project in English. After the last test I'm desperate."

"Which means," said Tony, "he has slipped to a B-minus."

"I'm leaving after fifth period. I'll call you from my brother's, okay?"

"If you want to."

Tony tugged on Mac's arm. "Say good-bye and let's get to lab."

Cory turned the other direction. Mac stopped her.

"Please don't get mad at me because you're hating someone else. They win that way, too. Promise?"

His glasses had slipped. Cory tapped her own nose to signal, and he pushed them up. "I promise," she said.

The next morning another white triangle was jammed into the door frame of her locker. Cory pulled it loose and unfolded it carefully, as if she expected filth to spill onto her hands.

Indians carry diseases.

Whores should be prepared.

She crumpled the paper and dropped it into her bag. She spun the lock around until it clicked and released. When she pulled open the gray door she felt something spill out and fall on her feet. People around her laughed. A mound of condom packets covered her shoes.

"Hey, I want some!" a voice called. Cory, forcing herself to crack through the anger and embarrassment, finally moved. She reached down, picked up a handful, and threw them with all the force she could muster. She did not scream.

"At least they weren't used," said Sasha.

"Ha ha," said Cory. She twisted the phone cord around her wrist. Sasha had been sick that day and had missed school. As soon as Cory reached home in the afternoon, she had called her with the story.

"But this is good because now we can figure out who's harassing you. All we have to do is track down who's been buying a lot of condoms. Who has your locker combination?"

"You."

"No way, Cory K."

"He probably just slipped them through the vents. It must have taken a long time. There are forty-three, not including the ones I threw down the hall. Evidently he has a favorite brand because they're all the same: Mighty Max, multicolored.

"Forty-three! What would that many cost?"

"I have no idea, Sasha."

"Do you still have them?"

Cory scooped up a handful of the foil squares. "Right here on the kitchen table."

"What did you tell your parents, that it was homework?"

"I haven't told them anything. They went to Wausau to the doctor and aren't back yet."

"Is something wrong?"

"A low fever that won't go away. It could be nothing, it could be serious."

"In case it's serious, here's some advice: don't leave the condoms on the table. Your mother's heart couldn't handle it."

After saying good-bye, Cory remained seated at the table and absently arranged the condoms in lines and circles. What would Mac say about this? She was glad he hadn't been there when she opened her locker. The embarrassment could have been fatal. As she debated how to tell him, the phone rang, and she smiled as she picked it up. She had thought of the perfect joke.

Mike's greeting was immediately chilling. They should have been returning home by now.

"Her doctor put her into the hospital for the night."

"Only a night?"

"I hope so, but he said that they might have to transfer her to Minneapolis to the transplant unit. He's worried she can't wait much longer. If there's no heart to harvest they'll have to put in an artificial one. He thinks an infection has set in, which could indicate organ failure."

With a mad mental dash, Cory recalled the heart specialist's warnings about infections: a weak heart is prone to bacteria, the bacteria weakens it further, the other organs don't get the blood they need, and the resulting organ failure, gone unchecked, is fatal.

"I'll come tonight."

"There's no need. Wait until tomorrow. Then we'll know more. Please let Rob know what's going on. We're in Room 257 if he wants to call."

"Okay." She pictured Rob upon hearing the news: any room he was in would suddenly be too small.

"Is everything there all right?" Mike asked.

She looked at the condoms. "Just fine. Everything's fine."

She called and left a message with her brother's wife. Then she cleared the table, sweeping the condoms into a bag. She took that to her room and had just finished stuffing it into the crowded sweater drawer of her bureau when the phone rang again. This time it was Mac.

In their rush to share news about his brother and her mother, she forgot about the surprise in her locker. Mac was especially concerned about her mother.

"I don't know if I should be here or there," he said. "With my brother or with you."

"You'll be home soon."

"Home? I guess so. Yeah, I'll be home soon."

That night Cory slept in the rollaway bed. It had the faint smell of perfume. She watched the fire burn low, and just before the last flame sank into embers she reached up, tapped the dream catcher, and sent it spinning.

Cory skipped school the next morning and drove to Wausau. At five past nine she pushed open the door to Room 257, nodded to her mother's roommate, and walked to the far bed. It was empty.

"They took her to intensive care at about seven-thirty," the roommate said.

Cory turned and raced out. Her mother's room was filled with busy white coats. One of them redirected Cory to the door.

"I'm her daughter," she protested.

"I'm her doctor," the coat said. "You must wait outside."

Cory found Mike in the lounge. "I skipped school," she said. "I just knew I should be here." He rubbed his unshaven face. She wondered if he'd heard her.

"Overnight," he said. "Overnight she turns blue and yellow. Blue from bad circulation, yellow from liver failure. That fast." Cory took his hand and they waited.

At eleven-seventeen, Margaret Knutson died of massive organ failure. When the doctor came to Cory's and Mike's chairs, kneeled, and told them, Cory checked her watch. Study hall. Her mother had died during study hall.

8

CORY GRABBED a handful of cloth and held her skirt down against her thigh. Twice already the wind had made it billow up, lifting the hem nearly to her chest and flashing the slip. If the minister didn't finish soon, they'd all be blown out of the cemetery.

Other women were also having trouble. Cory bit the inside of her cheeks to keep from laughing when she spotted one of the nursing home residents struggling with the wind. The woman's left hand was slapped against shiny black dress folds that threatened to balloon, while her right hand pinned a large hat to her head. A black purse swung from the raised hand and rhythmically batted the woman's face, nudging her glasses farther and farther out of place across the bridge of her nose. Finally, the woman gambled: she swiped her hand down and repositioned the glasses, then returned her hand to her head. The purse swung wildly with the sudden movement and knocked off her glasses.

The hat had already blown askew and was held precariously in place over her left ear by a single hatpin.

Cory turned to look elsewhere. The minister, drowned out by the wind, was saying something, a soundless intonation over the casket. It could likely be heard only in the Upper Peninsula. Probably more prayers, more blessings, more kind and hopeful words about her mother's soul. The minister had quite a lot to say about Margaret Knutson, though she had never met the woman. The local pastor was vacationing in Hawaii, and Mike had arranged for a substitute from another town. Cory released her bite and breathed deeply. Just get through it, she chanted silently. Just get through it. Once again she felt close to crying; once again she vowed she would not.

Mac had known she wouldn't want to cry, not in front of all the people. He had called every night from his brother's new place to see how she was doing. Yesterday he had offered again to return in time for the service.

"You're sweet, Mac," she'd replied. "But you don't have to. There are almost too many people around right now. Rob and his wife and Mike's kids and their families. I'll see you in school on Monday."

"Here's a suggestion," he said, "because I know you won't want to cry with all those people watching. You'd rather die first."

"Bad joke, Mac."

"Sorry, unintended. Okay — when you think you can't fight it anymore just look at the priest —"

"Pastor. When we're anything, we're Lutheran."

"Whatever. Just look at him and imagine he's doing the service wearing nothing but bikini briefs. It'll work. No way you can cry."

Women ministers were still uncommon around Summer, and Cory hadn't expected one today. Too bad Mac wasn't there to enjoy following his own advice. The fresh wave of grief subsided and Cory smirked through the remainder of the interment service. Twice the minister caught her eye and returned Cory's grin with a puzzled smile.

As soon as the final blessing was spoken, people turned and walked away. The March wind was cold and the prayers had gone on too long. Cory didn't linger either; she would come back soon on her own.

Alicia was walking hesitantly over the crusty snow toward the nursing home van. Cory caught up with her and took the woman's arm. Alicia smiled down at her.

"Thank you, dear. This ground is treacherous."

"Thank you for coming."

"Those of us who are still ambulatory never miss a funeral. And we did so care for your mother. Terrible day for a burial, though. The wind is nasty. I saw you try not to laugh when Winnie's hat nearly blew away. I told her not to wear a hat."

"Are you coming over to the house? Everyone's invited, and there's a ton of food."

"I think not. Church and a tramp through the snow are more than enough activity for us. Besides, it's almost time for afternoon medications. We can't miss our pills. We might up and die."

A nursing home aide was smoking a cigarette by the

van, and he flicked it into the snow as they approached. "Time to go back," he said. "You're the last one."

Alicia looked at Cory. The old woman's purple lips curved into a slight smile. "All these funerals. It sometimes feels like I *will* be the last one." She kissed Cory. "She was too young. I wish it had been me." Alicia waved away the aide and climbed by herself into the van. She sat down and stared straight ahead.

"Cory!"

She traced the call and saw Sasha and Tony waving from his car. She walked toward them, stopping several times to accept condolences and shake hands.

"Oh, man," she said to her friends when she finally reached them, "I'm starting to get depressed."

Sasha and Tony smiled at each other. "We thought so," said Sasha. "We have the remedy. Get in the car and we'll take you back to the house."

Cory looked for Mike and spotted him walking away from the gravesite. He had one arm around Rob and was holding his youngest grandchild in the other. She waved to catch his attention, then signaled her intention to leave with her friends. He lifted his arm from her brother and blew a kiss in reply.

Sasha followed Cory into the back seat. "That's right, leave me alone up here," said Tony as he started the car and drove away. "I don't get to drink and I sit all alone."

"Drink?" asked Cory. "Who's drinking?"

Sasha lifted aside a blanket on the floor to reveal a six-pack of beer. "We are. Pop a cold one." She twisted a can loose and handed it to Cory.

Cory rolled the sweaty can in her hands. "I don't do this."

"Neither do I. I don't even know what the stuff tastes like. But . . ." Sasha's voice cracked, and Cory looked at her. Tears were running down her cheeks. "But my best friend buried her mom today, and I didn't know what to do to make anything seem better." She wiped off the tears and snapped open her beer. "I was never taught to pray."

Cory snapped open her own beer and took a long drink. She liked it better as more went down.

Tony took them on a slow and meandering two-beer drive to Cory's house. By the time they arrived, cars had already filled the driveway and lined the side of the road that led to the house. Tony dropped them off and drove away to find a parking spot.

"Hold me up," said Cory.

"Nobody gets drunk on two beers," said Sasha. "Just remember that."

Mike opened the door. "It's about time."

Cory nodded. She didn't want to speak. He would know, instantly.

"Where have you been? People want to see you."

"Just driving around." She and Sasha got away quickly. "He knows," Cory whispered.

"Don't be silly."

"I'll be punished for this."

"Only when you get to hell. Now relax."

Two-beer drunk at her mother's funeral luncheon. Cory stood by the buffet table and concentrated on the display of food. The man next to her said something.

"That's nice," said Cory. "Thank you for coming."

The man looked confused and left with his plate of food. Sasha giggled.

"What's funny?"

"He just told you his sister died of the same heart disease as your mother. You said, 'That's nice.' It's obvious you had better eat something. Oh, no, here comes the minister."

"The bathroom, let's hide in the bathroom." They retreated quickly, elbowing their way through clumps of people and arriving at the bathroom just as Cory's sister-in-law was about to step inside.

"Emergency," Cory said. "Sorry."

Elaine pounded on the door after they closed it. "Don't take forever."

"Go upstairs," Cory shouted back. She and Sasha leaned against the door and laughed.

"We can't stay here forever."

"Two minutes if we're lucky." Cory turned on the cold water and splashed her face. "You have corrupted me. I will rot in hell."

"Probably. But at least you'll get through today."

"That's my motto: Just get through it."

"Cory!" Elaine pounded again.

"I said go upstairs."

"Someone named Mac is here and he's asking for you."

"Oh, oh," said Sasha.

81

Cory closed her eyes. "Wonderful. My boyfriend makes a surprise return from putting his alcoholic brother in a halfway house and he finds me drunk at my mother's funeral." She looked at Sasha. "Do you think he'll find it funny?"

"Two beers, Cory. Only two."

They left the bathroom. As she walked into the living room Cory took a peppermint from a candy dish on a table. Sasha left to find Tony.

Mac was standing in front of the fireplace, listening to Mr. Bartleby. They both turned to greet Cory. She nodded to her former boss and smiled at Mac. "This is a nice surprise."

"Barb called me last night and threatened to dump my things in a snowbank if I didn't get back today."

"An empty threat," said Mr. Bartleby. "The weather has been so warm that there are no snowbanks, just the usual layer of early March mush. Well, Cory, do you want your job back? I can offer a little raise. When fishing season opens, we'll be getting busy."

"Maybe I will do that, Mr. Bartleby. Thank you. I won't be needed around here anymore."

He kissed her on the cheek. "She was a sweet person, Cory. Let me know about the job." He left.

"I'm really glad to see you," Cory said to Mac.

He nodded slightly. "I talked to Tony. He said you and Sash put away most of a six-pack in twenty minutes."

Cory felt flushed but suddenly sober. "Don't disapprove. I don't think you have the right to disapprove."

"Is this sort of thing going to be a habit?"

She sucked on the last chip of peppermint, then let it slip down her throat. "Would you dump me if I said yes?"

"I think I would."

"Don't make me grovel in shame, Mac. It was a little bit of craziness on the crummiest day of my life."

He didn't answer. He put his hands in his pocket, took them out, then tightened the knot on his tie.

"You look nice," she said softly.

"I'm sorry I didn't wear a suit. I don't have one."

"Doesn't matter. You're perfect."

"No, I'm not."

"Am I forgiven?"

"After four days with my brother I guess I just didn't appreciate the timing of your 'little bit of craziness.' I'm sorry."

"Cory, I found you!"

Cory felt a gentle tug on her sleeve and turned. "Hello, Pastor Lunden."

"Hello, dear. I need to get back to Forest Lake, but I wanted to tell you how much I enjoyed meeting your family and how I wish I had known your mother. She certainly was loved. Who's this?"

"A friend of mine. Harvey MacNamara. Mac."

Cory stepped behind the minister. "Bikini briefs," she mouthed silently.

Mac's eyes widened. Cory could tell he was fighting back a smile. He offered his hand. "Pleased to meet you, Pastor Lunden."

"Oh, I do prefer first names. Kathleen, please." She

turned and hugged Cory. "I'll be thinking of you."
Then she was gone.

"And I'll be thinking of you," said Cory, "in bikini
briefs."

"My idea worked?"

"Perfectly, especially when I thought about how
you'd enjoy her preaching. I didn't shed a tear."

"You can, you know. It's okay." He stroked her
cheek with a finger. "I'm so sorry about your mother."
His voice cracked slightly, and he bit his lip.

Cory hugged him. She didn't care who might be
watching.

They decided to get food and found Sasha and Tony
grazing around the table. "I found him on the deck,"
said Sasha, "where your brother and his friends have
opened up a cooler of beer."

"Can you imagine? Beer on my mother's burial
day!"

"Whatever gets you through," said Mac. "Where's
Mike? I really should speak to him before I sit down
and eat."

"He took someone to the front deck," said Sasha,
"to show how he converted it to a three-season
porch."

Mac excused himself. "I'll be back in a minute."

"He is so polite," said Sasha as she watched him
work his way through the crowd.

"Has your brother met him yet?" Tony asked Cory.

"No. He knows I'm going with someone, but
they've never met."

"It might be interesting."

"What do you mean by that?"

Tony spooned ripe olives onto his plate. "Evidently the tribe has designated Summer Lake as a spearing site. The guys on the deck were pretty heated up."

"You mean your dad was," said Sasha.

Tony shrugged. "He's been the town racist for years and always gets wound up." He smiled at Sasha. "That's where I get it from."

"You didn't inherit that part, Tony," she said. "You have a good heart."

"They were talking about staging protests again," Tony went on. "Rob and some of the others have built up a head of steam. Does he know your boyfriend is an Indian?"

"I don't know. Maybe not."

"It might not be a bad idea to get him settled down before he actually meets Mac. Just a suggestion."

Cory went to find her brother. A large group of men had collected on the deck. They were all working on cans of beer. She stood behind her brother, waiting for him to finish an anecdote about the road crew that had the other men shaking their heads and swearing. Rob had gone to the barber the day before in preparation for the funeral. No more ponytail to tweak. When the story was finished, she tapped him on the shoulder. He saw her standing behind him, put down his beer, and hugged her tightly.

"It hasn't been too bad today, has it?" he said. "Good friends help."

"Rob, would you come inside? There's someone I want you to meet."

"Great news, Cory," he said as he followed her into the kitchen. "Fred Strickler says my name has come to the top of the hire list for the plant and that I should be taken on within a few weeks. Mike says we can move in here for a while. Lord Almighty, no more road tar and working in the sun. I'm coming home, kid." His face was radiant.

"That *is* good news, Rob. But you can't have my room for your weights."

"Won't need it. In a few months we'll have our own place. And then let the babies start rolling out!"

"You are sad, Robbie. Elaine's only twenty-one. Let her get a life first."

"She thinks I am her life."

His smiling face rekindled her sadness. "Rob, you look so much like Mom."

"No. She was never this pretty."

"That's true. You got it all didn't, you? Blond hair and curls. I can't believe you cut it off."

"I don't miss it."

"If you aren't going to wear the tail, maybe you should get an ear pierced. Something."

"Right. And have people think I'm queer?"

"That's old. No one thinks that anymore."

"I think that."

"Rob, I hope you're not turning into someone I don't like."

He frowned. "I'm your brother. How could that happen? Now, who am I supposed to meet? The new boyfriend?"

"His name is Mac."

"Wrong. His name is Harvey. I've heard about him."

"Did you hear that he's Indian?"

Rob sipped his beer. "I did. Lord, Cory, you always did like being different. Loud and different, that's my sister."

"Don't be ordinary, Rob. Don't be an ordinary Wisconsin redneck."

He raised his eyebrows. "A redneck?"

"I heard that all your beer buddies out there were screaming about the spearing. That's a Wisconsin redneck."

He sipped again. "Mike said the same thing. He said he's got Indian guests today and he didn't want them to hear it and *he* didn't want to hear it. He told us to keep it out of the house. Boy, Mom dies, and suddenly I feel like I've got a family of strangers." Rob looked behind her. "Hello. I bet you're the guy."

Cory turned and saw Mac. She hooked her arm through his and pulled him forward. "This," she said firmly to her brother, "is Mac. My boyfriend. And this," she said, reaching out and tapping Rob on the chin, "is my brother."

9

In 1837 and 1842 the Chippewa Indians living in northern Wisconsin signed two in a series of treaties with the United States government. In those treaties land was ceded to the federal government while the right to fish, hunt, harvest, and gather on the land was retained. In 1854 another treaty was signed. That one established permanent homelands, or reservations, for the Chippewa. For more than a hundred years, state and local authorities restricted Indian hunting, fishing, and rice harvesting to the reservations. In 1983 a federal court decision affirmed the Chippewas' right to take fish from lakes in all of the northern third of Wisconsin. Later decisions broadened this ruling to include hunting and harvesting rights. As the tribes in Wisconsin exercised their rights, especially the right to spear spawning fish in spring, an activity prohibited to the general public, there were protests by some of the white population of the state.

The Chippewa, however, were undeterred from reclaiming their rights.

Derived from the word Ojibwa, Chippewa is the legal name for the people who call themselves Anishinabeg — original people.

"Ojibwe, Ojibwa, Ojibway. Can't these people figure out what to call themselves?" Rob rolled up the newspaper he had been reading and smacked Cory on the rump as she walked by the kitchen table. She was in her bathrobe, just out of the shower. "What term does the boyfriend prefer?"

"His name is Mac. Anyway, he's Cree, so he's not the one to ask."

"Cree-ist Almighty, does it make a difference?"

"Not to a Neanderthal," said Elaine. Cory laughed and gave her sister-in-law a thumbs-up.

The back door opened and closed, and Mike shouted a greeting. A moment later he appeared in the kitchen and set a grocery bag on the counter. "Sorry I'm late. But I picked up some chicken and salad so we won't go hungry." He noticed Cory in her bathrobe. "I thought you were going to Sasha's tonight, but you look like you're going to bed."

"I showered and I'm waiting for my jeans to get out of the dryer."

He handed her some items from the bag to put away in the cupboard, then smiled at Rob and Elaine. "Was she in for the usual hour?"

Rob nodded. "There won't be hot water for a week."

Cory protested. "Not true. Anyway, it's almost impossible to get rid of the cleanser odor without a good soak, and I am not going out on a Saturday night smelling like disinfectant."

Rob rose from the table and started laying out place mats and napkins. "If you quit working at the motel, we could probably save your salary in hot water bills."

"I'm not going to quit, not a second time. It's kind of a crummy job, but it beats spending the whole weekend here." She quickly looked at Mike and wished she'd phrased it differently. He was gently bouncing a lettuce head in his hands.

He tossed it to her. She bobbled it, then secured it against her chest.

"I just mean the days seem kind of empty," she said to him.

"I know what you meant, Cory. And they are empty."

Rob opened the dishwasher and pulled out some clean silverware. "Not next Saturday. I guarantee a full agenda that day."

Mike's expression tightened. "Don't, Robbie. I haven't asked up until now, but now I am asking. Please don't go to the landing." Mike faced his stepson. "The law is clear. They have the right to spearfish. You and Jack Merrill and Clem Woodruff and the other noisemakers you enlist can go to the boat landing and protest forever, but all you will gain is a sorry reputation for yourself and the town. The law says you are wrong."

"The law is wrong. How can you have different rights for different people? Is that American?"

"The law —"

Rob pounded the broad ends of the silverware in his fist against the countertop. "All right, it's the law! Then the only option we have is to make them so god-damn uncomfortable they don't want to come to Summer Lake and spear. The town and the four resorts on that lake depend on business from fishermen. How many fish will be left to catch this summer if they're speared while spawning? How many?"

Elaine took the silverware out of her husband's hand. "I would guess that the fish population is in more danger from the motorboats and bad septic tanks at those four resorts than from three days of spearing," she said.

Rob looked at Cory, Mike, and Elaine in turn. "I'm all alone on this, aren't I?"

"Don't do it, Rob," Mike said softly. "Your mother —"

Rob slapped the counter. "Don't say that. She's not here and she has nothing to do with this."

The dryer buzzer sounded from the basement and Cory excused herself, happy to escape the anger. She had seen and heard enough.

The argument continued as she dressed in her room. Mike was right and Rob was wrong, but she was hesitant to join the fight. In the days following her mother's death, they had all been balancing too much — emotions, memories, emptiness, and the tiring business of living together. Cory feared that if everyone took sides and started fighting, the fragile balance would topple. So when Mike and Rob started in on the subject of spearing protests, she usually left the room or even found a reason to leave the house.

"He adopted you, didn't he?" asked Sasha. "That means he decided years ago that he always wants you in his life."

"What if he remarries? Where do I fit in? What if he and Rob start hating each other so much because of this spearing business that they turn away from each other? Where does that leave me?"

"At home with Mike. At least until you're eighteen."

"The saddest thing about it all is that they really love each other. But they have this difference, this huge difference, and they can't stop fighting about it. They could take a lesson from you and Tony."

"What have we done?"

"You're a flaming liberal, and he's a country redneck. You get along."

"He's not, really."

"Only because of you."

Sasha picked up a magazine from the floor and began flipping through it. "Oh, sad." She pointed to a swimsuit ad. "Are these women even human?" She flipped a few more pages. "It's too bad they can't reconcile things the way Antonio and I do."

"Why couldn't they? What's the secret?"

"Sex."

"Be serious."

Sasha ripped out a perfume insert and waved it around. "This stuff smells like my grandmother. And I *am* serious." She smiled. "Anything else you want to know?"

"When?"

"At night, mostly, like the rest of the world."

"I mean, when did you start?"

"Remember the spaghetti supper and how we had that fight? That night. We fight so easily sometimes. And when we were driving to my house after leaving the senior center, Tony got really down about who he is and who I am. Do you suppose they'll ever get back with the pizza?"

"Right now I don't care. What happened?"

"It's sort of like what you were talking about, wanting to find something to make the differences not matter. He was going on about them so much, about how his family is pure blue-collar and my dad is the plant's deputy v.p., how he's never been out of Wisconsin and I've traveled all over. It went on all the way home. He's right, of course. Sometimes there is this huge gulf."

"So now you share something."

"Don't disapprove, Cory."

"Do I look like I disapprove?"

"It's oozing out of every pore."

"Sash, I don't know what I think. Yes I do, okay? I think it's scary. But right now I think everything is a bit scary. Nothing's simple anymore." She stretched out a leg and prodded Sasha's hip with her foot. "Including our Saturday night doubles with you two.

Now I know we should leave early. You idiot, couldn't you have found a better way to not fight?"

Sasha rifled through the magazine pages. She looked up. "Don't be so judgmental."

"I'm just asking."

When the next page slipped through her fingers and fell open, Sasha tapped it with her fingers. "Look at this, Cory. This is it."

The black-and-white magazine picture was an advertisement for jeans. A bare-chested, slender young man wearing tight jeans had his finger hooked through a belt loop of his companion's equally tight jeans. The young woman's hands were resting on his chest.

"They're too gorgeous to be real," said Cory. "Nice and steamy, though. Do you suppose they are permanently joined at the pelvis?"

Sasha jabbed at the photo. "This is how I feel when I'm with Tony. This is how terrific it is to be with him. Cory, here's my life: I live with a stepmother only ten years older than me; I hardly ever hear from my own mother; I'm fifteen pounds overweight, and I get pimples on my butt. When I'm with Tony, though, I feel as good as this photo. About everything. And he does too. Nothing else makes me feel that good. I will not believe it's wrong."

"Sash, I hear you. But I still think it's a scary way to feel better about life."

"Do you have another answer?"

"No answer at all."

Sasha found another perfumed insert, leaned forward, and waved it across Cory's space. "Aren't you going to ask me what it's like?"

"I'm not totally ignorant."

"Not the least bit curious?"

"Obviously you want to tell me. Okay, Sasha, I'll ask. What's it like? Did it hurt? Do you leave the lights on? Does Tony make funny noises?"

"I'm not sure I want to tell you now."

Cory squeezed her soda can until it snapped and bent. "I'm sorry, Sash. I know I'm not being a very good friend, but it's hard sometimes to be happy about other people's happiness."

"I'll forgive you."

"I do want to know one thing: are you at least being careful?" Headlights panned the room as a car turned into the driveway.

"Usually."

Cory moaned. "Stupid, stupid."

"There's nothing rational about any of it, okay? You can't plan everything. After this winter, you should know that." She closed the magazine, and it slid off her lap. "Do you still have your stash?"

"My what?"

"The condoms. Rubbers, Tony's dad calls them. I hate that."

A back door opened, and the boys entered the house. They were singing the chorus of a pizza commercial.

"You can have them all. They're just taking up space in my dresser drawer. I've been waiting to find out who was doing that stuff and dump them in his locker."

"At least he stopped."

"Are you coming?" Tony called from the kitchen.

"Be right there," Sasha called back. They rose from their chairs and picked up their soda cans.

"I suppose he stopped because of Mom's dying."

"I'm surprised he had that much feeling."

Cory put her arm around Sasha. "Take them all."

"I don't need that many; it's not like we're sex machines. And you should keep some, just in case."

"No. Mac and I don't need that now."

Tony met them in the kitchen doorway. "Get in here. What's keeping you? Been talking about me, I bet."

Cory and Sasha smiled at each other. "Not exactly," said Sasha and she tugged on the frayed collar of his sweatshirt. "Just about the things you like to wear."

After eating too much pizza and losing at cards, Cory fell asleep during the video the boys had rented. Mac gently nudged her awake.

She sat up abruptly and pretended to be alert. "What have I missed?"

"Half a dozen dope dealers have been shot, all of them black. They'll probably start on the Hispanics next. I think I'd like to not watch any more."

"Let's go then. By the time I take you home and say good night, I'll be pushing curfew."

Tony and Sasha were sitting together on the sofa and didn't protest their departure. They seldom did, though Cory and Mac rarely stayed late. Cory now understood why.

She parked in Barb's driveway. A powerful spotlight

illuminated the ground in a huge circle. "Either I take out that light with a rock," said Mac, "or we don't do more than a quick kiss."

"We never do more than a quick kiss. And that's fine."

He set her hair in place behind her ear and traced her jaw line with his thumb. "Do you know what Tony told me tonight?"

"That they're having sex."

He put his hands in his lap. "Yeah. I guess some people like to play with fire. But we all do that in different ways."

"How do we do it?"

"You have to ask?"

She didn't. Whores and injuns.

He began humming in a rhythmic pattern of rising and falling notes. Cory suspected it was a drum song. Barb's husband, who sang with a drum circle, was teaching him. "Mac, is it hard on you having a white girlfriend?"

"Not when it's Cory K."

"Straight answer, please."

"I do hear about it from some of the other kids. I was surprised. I've never lived anyplace before where such a clear race line was drawn."

"What do they say?"

"Aren't Indian girls good enough for me? Am I trying to be white? That sort of thing. It was especially hard when you were getting those notes."

"At least that's stopped."

"I wonder why. Maybe he, or she, just got scared

of getting caught. No, it's not really hard, Cory. I suppose if I had actually planned it, maybe I wouldn't have picked a popular white girl whose life is running upside down."

She took his hand.

"I didn't plan a darn thing. And I'm happy. Now, how about that quick kiss?"

A late-night drive home on a country road had long been Cory's favorite way to end the day. Thoughts came tumbling out of nowhere while the radio pulled in music and talk from distant places. Tonight a radio shrink out of Oklahoma was fixing things between a woman and her mother. "Talk to each other!" the doctor urged. "Talk and then talk some more!" Cory hit the scan button and let it run. Spring training baseball, news, music, more baseball — all in four-second patches. She turned off the radio.

"Talk to each other!" she said, mimicking the radio doctor. Nice advice, but she couldn't do it, not now. What talking she and her mother had done would have to last a lifetime. No more conversations by the lake or on the porch or in the glow of a dying fire. But already she needed more — needed to know more, to hear more from her mother. Cory made a mental list of things she wished she could ask. Will Rob and Mike stop fighting? Is Sasha being stupid? Will Mac want to play with fire? How old were you the first time? Was it with my father?

The unanswered questions hung suspended in the rumbling rhythm of the speeding car.

Rob was sitting on the deck when she returned

home. He patted the empty chair next to his, and she sat down. "You're back early."

"It's nearly eleven and that's my curfew. How are things here?"

"We quit fighting, if that's what you mean. Even played some gin. I won two bucks." He put his feet up on the deck rail. "It's great out, isn't it? You can really feel some spring warmth in that breeze. Six more days and it's April. Look at that sky, Cory. You never see a sky like that anywhere but around here. Gosh, I'm glad to be home."

Cory didn't want to dampen her brother's spirits. Not all that long ago she would have let him have it with both barrels. Would have let him know everything she thought about everything he did. But something had been sucked out of her when her mother died and she was mute. So, she didn't accuse him of stupidity or bigotry or simply being wrong, but just sat quietly alongside her cheerful brother and together they stared up at the star-dense sky.

A gust of wind blew across them. Cory zipped up her jacket and shoved her hands in her pocket. "Darn," she whispered.

"What's wrong?"

Cory pulled out the ring of motel keys. "I left work in a hurry. Mr. B. was threatening to tell me about his father's surgery. I got out as fast as I could."

"Bartleby is a good guy. He's on our side."

"Rob, there shouldn't be sides. You must know how Mom —"

"Shut up, Cory." He gripped the arm of her chair

and shook it. "I wish you and Mike wouldn't bring her into this." They sat again in silence. A nighthawk flew across the moon, creating a momentary eclipse of the pearl white circle.

"When he mentions her, he's only trying to stop me by laying on a guilt trip. He's trying to turn the protest into another disappointment to her, just another one of Robbie's screwups."

"You haven't been a screwup," Cory said softly.

"You're seven years younger and don't know half of what's gone on in this family." He counted off on his fingers. "There was my suspension in eighth grade."

"I never knew about that. For what?"

"Hiding Derek Winters's clothes in gym three days running. They finally found out who did it." He tapped another finger. "Shooting out the lights on Main Street with my BB gun."

"I remember that."

"My DWI. My only DWI. Of course, I was fifteen and unlicensed for the 'D' part of it."

"I'm beginning to think screwup might be a good term."

"The biggie, of course, was Amy Tilghman's abortion. That hurt her the most, I know."

"What? You didn't even go with her."

"You're still a little innocent, aren't you? For your information, Cory, you don't have to *go* with someone. Just *be* with them at the right time."

"Wrong time, I'd say. An abortion?"

"Senior year. We skipped school one day that fall

100

and went to Madison and back. One very long day. She ended up telling her mom, who told our mom. That was quite a scene when she confronted me." He retied a sneaker. "Mom wasn't happy, I'll say that. Remember how she would yell about the little stuff like forgetting to take out the garbage, but on a major wrong she'd just get solemn and soft-spoken?"

"I remember."

"Well, she was practically whispering that time. Said how wrong she thought it all was. How she was disappointed that I'd become a boy who was so thoughtless about girls and hadn't even been careful. Said if we weren't ready to be parents we weren't ready for sex. It was quite a lecture. But it stuck with me, I guess. Since then I've only been with Elaine. Damn careful, too." He glanced over. His expression was partially hidden in shadow, but his eyes were highlighted by moonlight. They searched her. "How about you. Are you being careful?"

"It's not even close to being an issue."

"Good. Listen: if anyone plays cheap with you, I kill him."

Her hands were chilled and she tucked them under her thighs. "That's a pretty sexist attitude, big brother. I don't need your protection."

"I mean it."

His tension was overpowering. She reached across hesitantly and rubbed one of his hands, her thumb stroking back and forth and bumping over his large high school class ring. "Ease up, Rob. There is no one you have to hate."

"Cory, I'm just so mad about her dying! That's what it is, of course." He withdrew his hand. "I guess I need to start work. There has been too much sitting around and waiting. Ten more days and then I'm on at the plant."

"You can pass the time by working with me. I've seen you scrub out toilets plenty of times." She checked her watch. "Which is what I'll be doing in approximately nine hours. Time for bed." She rose and kissed him. "Coming in?"

"Not yet. Sleep tight, Sis."

Cory walked across the dark kitchen. A long finger of moonlight stretched in through a window and revealed a mess of playing cards and drinking glasses on the table. She stopped where the kitchen opened onto the living room. The living room fireplace framed a few embers. She stared at the orange glow, mesmerized by the wavering patterns of light. The surrounding stillness was complete.

A log collapsed and broke in half. Sparks shot up, then a final flame. Out of the corner of her eye Cory saw a golden flash. She turned and saw the dream catcher hanging from the wall over empty space.

10

CORY SPOTTED the white paper as soon as she turned into the hallway. She halted and was bumped several times by students hurrying to their lockers before leaving school for the weekend. When she resumed walking, it was in a slow and wary approach.

She pulled the paper out of the crack and looked behind her at the crowd of students. They were all intent on their business. She wished that just one person would stop and be caught by the horror of what she was holding.

She unfolded the paper. It was a printed poster with a grotesque characterization outlined in red. A cartoon Indian. At the bottom of the page were the date and time for the spearing protest at Summer Lake landing. Saturday, six P.M. Across the cartoon face were two bold red words: Spear This. Her correspondent had altered the printed message. "Spear" was crossed out and scrawled above was a familiar obscenity.

"Not again!" Sasha's voice cut through Cory's trance. Sasha grabbed the paper and scanned it. "This is awful. This is worse than anything I've ever seen." She waved it over her head and shouted. "Who did this? Who the hell did this?" The crowd slowed down and people looked up from their lockers and conversations, but no one stopped. "Someone knows," she continued. "One of you had to see something. Who is it?" She tore the poster into shreds and tossed it over the hallway. A few girls protested when paper bits landed in their hair.

Cory put all her books in her locker. "That was nice, Sasha. A little loud, but nice."

"Let's go to Donaldson's office now and tell him. You have to complain. You have to insist that he make a statement to the student body."

"Do I have to tell him about the condoms?"

"Tell him everything. Fight back, Cory. Why don't you want to fight back? That's not like you." She spun her lock, missed the release number, and started again.

Cory secured her lock and picked up her bag. "*I'm* not like me, okay?" She didn't wait for an answer but walked away.

Sasha caught up with her at the parking lot. "I really think you should tell Donaldson."

"What can he do besides sound grumpy over the P.A.? It's kind of perverse, but I'm almost glad this stuff has happened."

"How can you say that?"

"Mac has put up with harassment all his life. Now

104

I know a little bit, a very little bit, of what he's gone through."

"That's positive, I guess. But I wish I could fix it all for you. Just make it all stop and be better." Sasha's outrage was centered on her face in a fierce scowl.

Cory stopped and hugged her friend. "Thanks, Sash."

The scowl gave way to a smile. "Careful, you don't want to invite gay-bashing next."

They reached Cory's car. "I'll give you a ride home."

"No thanks. Six blocks twice a day is all the exercise I get." She dropped her book bag on the car hood. "Don't you wonder who's doing it?"

Cory unlocked the car door. "Sure. It could be almost anyone. Not you, not Tony. Although a year ago . . ."

"True enough. That's hopeful, isn't it? People do change. I think" — she paused and checked for anyone loitering between the few remaining cars — "maybe Nick and Karin."

Cory shook her head vigorously. "If it is, I don't want to know. Karin and I were Brownies together."

A car went past and honked. They waved absently and stepped back to avoid the spray as the car ran through a puddle.

"Have you by any chance changed your mind about going to the landing tomorrow night?"

"I'm not going, Sash. I can't be part of it."

"We need more people to show support for the spearing. We can't let the only ones from town be the protesters. I've heard that television crews from Milwaukee and Minneapolis might be there."

"And you know what they'll see? A few guys standing in a boat spearing fish and a bunch of other people shouting at each other. Will it help anything for me to come and take sides? Remember, I'd be shouting back at my brother. My brother. I suppose that's exactly what a reporter would love to see: 'Family Divided; report at six.'"

"Mac might be there."

"And I won't be. I've told him that and he accepts it. He said he wouldn't stay the entire evening. We plan to meet later on." She got in the car. Sasha tapped on the window, and Cory rolled it down.

"I wish you would come, but I understand." She gripped the door handle. "Cory K., I think you have been so great this winter with all you've gone through. Really strong."

"I don't feel that way."

"Probably not."

Cory stacked the cassettes that were scattered across the car seat, then toppled the pile with a finger poke. "Sash, too many things have happened too fast. I feel like I've been playing football or something and I got hit from behind. Bam! And all the wind has been knocked out of me."

Sasha laughed.

"It's not funny."

"Sure it is. You play football? You'd be crunched in a minute. But it explains why you're so quiet these days. If things were normal, that would have been you waving the poster and screaming." Sasha drummed on the car roof with her fingers. "Call me tomorrow if

106

you change your mind. I'd rather not go alone." She picked up her book bag, waved, and walked away.

Cory drove across the parking lot in the opposite direction. She slipped a tape into the player and punched the rewind button. While the tape whirred, Sasha's words replayed in her mind. "Wrong, Sash. Very wrong," she said tersely. She didn't feel strong. Not strong at all.

The next day there were posters in every one of the motel rooms. When Cory walked into the first room of the morning she was stopped cold at the sight of the flyer.

"Bartleby's on our side," she recalled Rob saying.

"And I'm not," she said firmly and ripped it down.

Ten rooms and twenty beds later she walked into the office with an armload of dirty laundry. A crowd of people was gathered around a large coffee urn that had been set out, an unusual measure of hospitality for the motel owner. Cory wished herself invisible as she plowed through the people with her overstuffed bag of sheets and towels. Mr. Bartleby followed her into the back room.

"We're absolutely full, Cory. The best weekend we've had since Labor Day. I've been turning away people for an hour now."

Laughter surged in the other room and Cory heard traces of conversation.

"How many spearers does it take . . ."

"Put two drunk Indians and two hungry bears . . ."

She opened her closet and slammed the linens into the bin. Mr. Bartleby was right behind her.

"It's too bad we can't rent out Unit 26. If I didn't charge full rate, do you think it would be okay?"

"The tub leaks and the bathroom tile is ripped up. No, I don't think it would be okay." She faced Mr. Bartleby. "By the way, I've been taking down those protest posters in the rooms. I'm sure you don't want that racist crap in your motel."

His hand started its up-and-down motion on his belly and continued stroking as he walked out of the room. A moment later he returned with a stack of posters and a roll of tape. "Put them up, Cory. I want them up."

"I *clean* rooms."

"I'm your boss, Cory. I say put them up."

"No."

"I want you —"

"I quit. I quit, Mr. Bartleby." She grabbed her jacket and slammed the closet door.

"Cory, the rooms aren't finished."

She walked into the office. "I quit," she said loud enough to silence the talking. "I can't work for a bigot."

Mike was alone in the house when she returned home. He looked up from the newspaper he had been reading as he ate lunch. He folded the paper and sipped some coffee, then pointed to the chair next to his. Cory sat down.

"Brad Bartleby called. He wants you to drop off the motel keys the next time you're in town."

Cory checked her jacket pockets. Empty. She patted the pouch of her sweatshirt, and the keys shifted and jangled. She pulled them out, twirled them twice around her thumb, and stuffed the ring into her jacket pocket. "I left in a hurry."

"He said that this time you can't have your job back. This time you quit for good."

"As if I would want it back."

"He told me what happened. I told him I thought you were right. He hung up on me." Mike crumpled his napkin and dropped it into his coffee cup. Cory could see the brown liquid travel upward through the paper. Mike pushed his chair back and looked at the ceiling. "Brad and I were lab partners in high school chem. I used to let him steal answers from me during tests." He rose and cleared his dishes.

"Where are Rob and Elaine?"

Mike sat back down. He didn't answer but sat still with his hands folded between his legs. He stared at the floor.

"Mike?"

He looked up with a jerk, as if suddenly pulled back from some better place.

"Rob and Elaine?"

"I kicked them out this morning. Well, not Elaine. She's always welcome."

"You kicked my brother out?"

"My stepson, Cory. He means plenty to me, too. But I told him that if he insisted on being part of that nonsense at the landing he couldn't live in this house. He's gone, Cory. I kicked Robbie out. Three goddamn weeks after Margaret dies and I kick her son out." He rose and immediately sat back down. "I'm getting out of here. I'm leaving."

Cory felt all warmth drain away.

Mike raised his hands and then let them drop on the table. "Cory, not like that. Just for tonight."

"Where are you going? And why?"

"To my son's. I don't want to be here when all the people in this town who were so wonderful to your mother turn on themselves. I don't want to be here when Robbie stops thinking and goes too far. He will, you know. He'll do it, unless Elaine can stop him or he gets hurt first. I don't want to be here when the sheriff calls and asks me to bail my stepson out of jail. Because I won't do it." He pulled his wallet out of his hip pocket. "You might need some money while I'm gone."

Cory watched him set down some bills. "Thirty bucks? Are you sure you're going for only one night?"

"Cory, I'm not leaving you. I'm just getting out while the town goes mad." He pressed his hand against the table and tapped his index finger several times. "On my first date with your mother, we went to a party at the Schneemans'. I was pretty pleased that Margaret had gone with me because no one had gotten her to go out since your dad died. I was the first, and I wanted to impress her. There was a big crowd there, and I started telling stories and jokes. And I told a couple of drunk Indian jokes. You know the kind. I remember that people were laughing so hard, drinks got spilled and Amy Schneeman sent us outside. When I took your mother home I asked her out again. I was certain no woman in the world would refuse me. She said, 'I can handle your cigarettes, but I don't like your jokes.' It took another three months and some

110

promises before she agreed to go out again. I remember . . ." He sank silently into the unfinished sentence.

"Remember what?"

He wiped a tear from the corner of his eye. "She had this thing, this idea that if you could change someone's heart —"

"You could change the world."

"You heard it too? Your mother's very own theory of revolution. She changed mine. I just wish she'd had more time to work on Robbie's. She would hate all this. And now that I've slammed the door on her son, she'd probably hate me, too."

"I don't think so."

"Why don't you come with me tonight?"

"I want to be around. Mac and I have plans." She picked up the bills and waved them. "Is this enough to bail Robbie out if he gets in trouble?"

"Not after you and Mac get pizza and a movie. Which is what I hope you have planned for tonight." He rose and folded his arms and looked down at her. "I don't feel good about going, Cory. I don't like leaving you alone."

"Hey, old man, it's fine. May I use the car?"

"It's yours. Just stay away from Dawn's store."

After he left, Cory fixed a small lunch and ate only a little of it. She cleaned her room, debated about doing the laundry, and instead took a bath. She soaked for a luxurious half hour in the steamy tub, replenishing the hot water every five minutes. When she at last forced herself to get out, she was soft, wrinkled, and sleepy. And it was only four P.M.

111

The silence in the house was absolute. No ticking clock, no blaring radio, no distant and faint mother's laugh from another room. Cory sat on the sofa and hugged a pillow. Looking out the window through the bare branches of the birches and maples, she could see down to the small lake at the edge of the property. The ice was already gone and the water sparkled diamonds on blue steel. It offered what Cory knew was only an illusory beauty, a false temptation to dive in; it was still dangerously frigid.

Her eyes tired from the sun's glare and she turned her attention to the quiet room. She picked up the family photo displayed on the table next to the sofa. It had been taken on Rob's wedding day. The four of them were overdressed and smiling. Cory grimaced and avoided looking at herself in the picture; she'd hated the lilac bridesmaid's dress with its frills and ruffles. She traced an X over her mother's face. Gone. An X over Rob. Gone. She breathed in the stillness of the house and traced an X over Mike. Gone. Maybe just for now, but if he was so quick to run off this time, so quick to throw out Rob, it might not be long before he found a reason to slam the door on her, too.

"Not much of a family anymore," she whispered. "Damn you, Rob. It's your fault. She's dead, and now you're killing the rest of us."

She had to stop him. She checked her watch. The protest wouldn't start for an hour, but she suspected that Rob, anxious and angry, was already at the landing. If she could make him leave, things might be patched up. They might yet have a family.

11

SUMMER LAKE was a popular destination for tourists and sportsmen because of its combination of sandy beaches and picturesque rocky shoreline, its clean water, and its bait-biting fish. The town of Summer was on the western shore of the nearly round lake. The public-access landing, where cabin owners and day visitors put in their boats, was on the northern shore. Most of the land surrounding the lake was in a state forest and undeveloped. A county road circled the lake, veering in and away from the water as high ground or swampy backwaters dictated. The nearest Indian reservation was twenty miles north.

Cory signaled to turn from the highway onto the gravel access road. A sheriff's deputy waved her over. She rolled down her window as he approached.

"You won't get much closer, young lady. Park where you can and be prepared to walk."

"It's Cory Knutson, Mr. Hartsoe."

"Sweetheart, I'm sorry. I've seen so many faces in such a short time that I guess I've quit looking."

"Have you seen Rob?"

"No, but that doesn't mean he's not there. I came on duty an hour ago when the sheriff called in all deputies. Five are working the crowd down at the landing."

Another car pulled in behind Cory's and was waved down. Cory backed up and around the car and took the nearest parking spot. As she inched into the opening she heard the branches and leaves of ditch shrubs scrape against the car doors.

Jogging a quarter mile was no challenge and she covered the distance quickly. She stopped just before the road veered right for a hairpin turn around a towering pine. Signs of a crowd were everywhere: gum wrappers and cigarette butts littered the ground, and hundreds of footprints obliterated the customary tire and animal tracks on the road.

People beyond the bend were shouting. The words were indecipherable to Cory, but the tone and tenor were clear. It was a taunting chant, broken occasionally by a rogue burst of invective and obscenity. Cory walked hesitantly forward.

The size of the crowd took her breath away. Three hundred, four hundred, too many to count accurately. A deputy motioned her to get in place behind a long cordon. Cory shook her head, stepped back, and leaned against a tree.

A mob pushed against the cordon, a sea of individual faces blurred into a single angry mob. And all of its noise and energy was directed at a much smaller group standing nearer the water. Those people, mostly Native Americans, but with several white companions, were formed loosely in a horseshoe that opened onto the waterfront. In the center four men sat around a drum. They lifted their sticks to begin a song and with the first beat were immediately answered by the protesters with the high-pitched, repetitive rasping of snare drums.

Cory heard several voices urging her to take a place behind the rope. She shook her head as she scanned the crowd for Rob. She saw Tony's dad lean over the rope and shout. His neck tensed into thick cords and his eyes bulged. She saw Sue Wilkins, her third-grade teacher; Pete Mickelson, the school librarian; Ben Robinson, Joshua Lane, Leslie Furman, Betsy Kelly, Thelma Ray. She could almost make a list of everyone she'd ever met in her life. Mike was right: the very people who had unhesitatingly helped when their family was in trouble were now snarling and yapping like fevered dogs.

"Cory!" Sasha's shout reached her through the noise. Cory saw her friend down by the water, arms waving above her head. Boos and curses followed Cory as she walked from the crowd to the smaller group. She recognized only a few people here and nodded to them. She knew Peter Rosebear and Roxanne's husband and a few of the others. The rest were strangers. The drumming ceased and the conversation swelled.

Sasha hugged her. "I just knew you would come.

Let me introduce you to the other witnesses. That's what they call us, witnesses."

Dim-witness, Cory wanted to respond. She was, she realized, angry at everyone. But she didn't want it to show. Not here. "I was taught," she said with false cheer, "that too much noise scares away fish. Why are they even going to bother going out in the boat?"

Peter overheard her. "Noise scares fish, but not fishermen. I'm glad to see you, Cory. Too bad Mike didn't want to join us."

I'm not joining you, she almost said. "I just came to find my brother."

Peter laughed. "You won't find him here." His arm swept toward the mob. "That's the place. Good luck."

Cory hooked her arm through Sasha's and whispered. "Has Mac been here?"

"Come and gone already. He said you two were meeting at the café at seven. I couldn't believe it — going on an ordinary date when he could be here. What a cop-out. I'm really disappointed in him. I can understand you not getting involved, but he should care."

The anger in the air was virulent and infectious. An airborne disease. Cory pulled her arm loose with a jerk. "That's racist, Sasha Hunter," she snapped. "Just because he's Indian you think he has to be here? And what right do you have to be disappointed?"

She left without giving Sasha a chance to answer. Cory walked across the wide sandy landing and was accosted by a deputy.

"Get behind the rope, girl, or I'll haul you out of here."

"I'll haul myself out of here," she said, still angry at everyone.

The deputy didn't like her voice. He tapped his club on her shoulder. "We don't want trouble tonight, and trouble sometimes begins with the mouth. Now get behind that rope." He walked away and left Cory standing alone in the neutral ground.

She saw Rob. He was with a man she didn't recognize, and their heads were bowed together. She doubted that they were praying. Cory ducked under the rope and edged through. Several hands patted her back in welcome. She shrugged them off when she could, but there were too many people in too small a space. She had never felt shorter.

She reached Rob and punched his arm. He looked at her but didn't speak. He was trying to understand why she was there.

"They're putting the boat in the water!" That cry was a signal for the mob to increase the volume of its chanting. The snare drum resumed its mocking rat-a-tat-tat.

Rob continued staring at Cory. She was again struck by the resemblance to their mother and was compelled to touch him. As she laid her hand on his cheek, she was bumped from behind. Her hand slipped, and two fingers jabbed his eye. He pressed his fist against the eye socket and doubled over.

"Geez, Cory, why did you do that?"

"It was an accident, Robbie." They were shouting, the only way to be heard. She started laughing, but a few tears rolled down. Laughing or crying, it didn't make much difference when nothing was making sense. "Robbie, leave with me. Everything's so screwed up, but if Mike knows you left it might end up okay."

He straightened and looked at her. One eye was red, watery, and twitching. "I can't believe you came to tell me that. I can't believe we're talking about this here."

"Maybe it was a dumb idea. But I thought I could make you care enough. About the family, Rob."

"Cory," he screamed. "This is a protest, not family counseling!" He lowered his face to hers. "And I was the one who was kicked out. What the hell does our stepfather care about the family? Tell me that."

She was bumped again and their heads crashed. Cory swore and Rob laughed. "Sis, this isn't the place. But why don't you stay?"

"It makes me sick."

"You and my wife." He rejoined the noisemaking. He raised his arms to punch fists into the air, and his jacket pulled up. Cory saw a handgun tucked into his belt.

She pounded on his arm. "You idiot, you have a gun. You have a fucking gun." She reached for it and he grabbed her arm.

"Don't be stupid, Cory. It just has blanks. A noise-maker, that's all."

She pulled her arm loose and left him.

The crowd noises followed her back to the highway. The shouts, the snare drum, the imagined pistol shots reverberated even after she was sitting in the car. She pushed a tape into the player and let it roar at full volume. While she laid her head back against the car seat and caught her breath, tears laid stinging tracks down her cheeks.

Seestadt's Café boasted the best malts anywhere, and usually on Saturday night quite a few were being sold. Cory often met Mac there in order to avoid the certain teasing and relentless questioning she'd face at Barb's house from the three girls.

Otto Seestadt was alone and counting bills at the register when Cory walked in. He lifted a hand to caution her not to speak until he was finished. She took a counter seat, swiveled slightly, and waited.

"You're early," he said as he wrapped a rubber band around a thin stack of bills. "Mac said seven."

"When was he here?"

"He left ten minutes ago. He said to tell you he'd meet you at the park. He had a bit of trouble when he was here, and I don't think he wanted to hang around and wait for more."

"Trouble?"

"Some dirt brains were hassling him." Otto rested his hairy arms on the counter and hunched over them. "It's not a good night to be an Indian in Summer. I threw the jerks out. Told them their party was at the landing. Then Mac left, too. Do you want a coffee or a cocoa? It's on the house, sweetheart."

Sweetheart, twice already. Cory wondered if she looked especially young tonight. "No thanks. But we might be back for some supper. I could use a licorice malt."

Otto shook his head. "You'll have to settle for pizza

from Jasper's place. Now that I've relayed the message to you, I'm closing up and going home. I can't explain it, Cory, but I don't like what I feel in the air."

Cory felt no warmth when she stepped outside. Early April nights were like that — a twelve-hour return to winter after a day's teasing spring weather. She didn't doubt that by morning a veneer of ice would cover the smaller lakes. But Otto was right: tonight there was a stranger, deeper chill.

Harold Bjornson Memorial Park was a two-table, three-swing clearing at the end of Main Street next to Bartleby's Inn. Cory's headlights panned the park as she pulled into the gravel lot. The sun had just set, leaving behind a wash of unreliable light, and she didn't see anyone until a shadow rolled out from behind one of the picnic tables and approached her car. It was Mac.

Cory ran to him. "Were you playing hide-and-seek?"

He didn't answer but stopped and cupped his face.

"Mac, what's wrong?" When she reached him, she sucked in air with a loud gasp. She reached for his hand, but pulled away when she felt its moist stickiness.

"These bastards in a car threw bottles at me when I was walking down here. One of them broke on a lamppost and a piece of glass got my forehead. I've been under the table, trying to stop the bleeding and trying to stay out of sight. Do you have any clean cloth or rags in your car? I've already soaked my sleeve."

Even without light she could see that his face was a

mess. "I don't have anything. Let's go to Barb's and clean you up."

"No." He swiped his face and flicked blood off his hand. "Barb had a terrible time keeping Jeff home from the landing. He's pretty hotheaded and she was certain he would lose it and go after some protester. If he sees me he'll be out the door looking for a fight. We can't go there."

"Let's find Doc Scudder."

"And explain what happened? He'd report it to the sheriff. I don't want to mess with cops tonight, Cory. Anyway, I don't think it's deep, just bloody. Take me to your place and I'll clean up there."

"Bleeding for five miles in my mother's car? Mike just cleaned it."

"Cory," he barked. "I'm bleeding buckets! Too bad about the damn car."

She had never liked anyone yelling at her, even for good reason. Cory stepped back, set her jaw, and shoved her hands into her jacket pockets. Her right knuckles grazed against cool steel.

"Wait a minute," she said. "I know what we can do."

Unit 26 was on the second floor overlooking the back lot of Bartleby's Inn. Cory inserted the master key into the lock and pushed as soon as she heard the click. She hoped Mr. Bartleby hadn't rented the room.

She pulled the heavy drapes closed and switched on a bedside lamp. Mac whistled. "Is this what a room looks like after you've cleaned it?"

Cory blew white dust off the television. "This is construction mess. The bathroom is being repaired." When she faced him she was nearly felled by sudden lightheadedness. She'd never seen so much blood. "Mac, you look awful. We're going to the doctor. Now."

"Let me clean up first and look at the cut. The forehead is a bloody spot. Barb's kids have been cut there and didn't need stitches. I bet I don't." He looked around. "Are you sure this is okay?"

"It's not okay, but no one is going to find out. Anyway, we'll mess up the bigot's linens and let him pay for cleaning. You lie on the bed. I'll get a washcloth."

Mac lay down. "I heard at the café that you had quit your job. I also heard why. Good move, Cory."

"You might not think so," she said as she walked to the bathroom, "when my money runs out and I make you buy all the pizzas."

There were no bath linens. Cory turned the tap and reddish water exploded out before settling into a clear stream. "At least the plumbing's working," she called. She returned to the other room and sat next to Mac on the bed. A smile was evident under the hand that he held pressed against his face.

"This is my very first time in a motel room with a girl. So romantic."

"I hear violins. Lift your head a minute." He obeyed, and she pulled out the pillow and removed the crisp white case. "I'll use this."

He repositioned the pillow and set his head back down. He closed his eyes and sighed. "I was so glad

to see you drive into that park. I was getting scared."
She kissed a clear spot on his cheek.

When she returned with the wet pillowcase he was sitting up. He was stripped to the waist. "Don't panic. The sleeve was kind of wet and sticky. That's why I took it off."

"Like you're really attractive now, anyway." He lowered his hand from the wound and Cory swooned again. She wanted to cry.

Blood bubbled slowly from a line above his left eyebrow. More blood, congealed and dried, was smeared across his face and streaked down his neck. Cory took a breath to steady her stomach and began wiping away the mess. Mac closed his eyes and relaxed.

"I think you're right," she said after she wiped the forehead. "It's not that deep and the bleeding has slowed." She finished cleaning his face and started on his neck. "This needs to be rinsed off. Just a minute." When she returned she handed the cloth to Mac. "You do the rest."

While he wiped his neck and chest she sat and looked at a painting on the near wall. Children picking yellow flowers under a blue sky, mothers with teacups in the background.

"What a lousy day," she said. "Do you know what happened? Mike kicked Rob out, then left to spend the night at his son's. Mac, I don't have anyone to go home to. It's empty."

His hand dropped onto her shoulder and began gently massaging. "I hate to see you like this," he said.

"You're the one who's a pulpy mess."

He drew up his knees and draped the cloth over them. The blood had stained it in abstract patterns of varying shades of red. "I should dry this and frame it," he said. "Give it one of those artsy ironic titles, like *Spring Spearing*."

"Throw it away. And that shoulder rub felt good."

He resumed the massage. "Last winter when I moved to Summer and started school, within two hours of first walking into the building I knew who Cory Knutson was."

"How did that happen?"

"There was an assembly that morning. You represented the student council when it presented all those dirty books to the school library."

"Not dirty books. They had been banned in other schools, and we thought Summer High should own them all."

"You were really funny. That's how I knew who you were. Then I'd see you in the halls or in the lunchroom, and it was like you were the happiest person in the world. Always. When you showed up at the powwow it blew me away. I couldn't believe it: Cory Knutson, School Star, hanging out with Indians. I just had to talk to you."

She shifted so she was facing him. She pulled up her right leg and let the knee rest on his chest. "Did I ever tell you that I was forced to go that night?"

"Many times, Cory. Many times." He stroked her knee with his thumb and it jerked.

"That's kind of a ticklish spot, Mac." He did it

124

again, and she clamped his hand down with her own. "Not funny."

"Ticklish anywhere else?"

"You'll have to find out."

"I just wish you weren't so sad." They both knew there was no answer to his wish. Mac reached out and turned off the bedside lamp. Cory lay down beside him. She kissed his bare shoulder.

A chorus of bleating car horns startled them. The noise crescendoed as a succession of vehicles roared past the hotel on the highway, accompanied by an undercurrent of screams and laughter. As the last car passed, an isolated and triumphant yell emerged from the discord: "Spear a redskin tonight!" The shouting and honking moved into the distance.

"I'm glad," Mac said, "that I'm not on the street."

Cory kissed him again, and he shifted to pull her closer.

"I'm alone with my boyfriend in a motel room," said Cory. "What happens next?"

Mac's hand stroked her arm. He kissed her again. "I know what I want."

Cory leaned forward and tugged the edge of the spread that lay folded across the foot of the bed. She pulled it over them, then resettled in his arms. "What do you want?" she said softly, eyes closed, mind at peace, heart beating at double time.

"An aspirin. My head really hurts."

Cory sat up. Her heart resumed a normal pace. "I don't have any, but I'll take you home."

"Not yet. I'd just get a million questions from the girls. Let's at least wait until Barb and Jeff have put them to bed." He pulled her back. "It's nice here; it feels safe."

Cory didn't feel safe at all. Tucked under his arm, she sensed a peeling away of all resolve and reason. If his hand moved across her chest, or his lips touched hers, she knew everything else would give way. She held still. It would be his move.

Mac giggled. Cory's spell broke. "What's the joke?" she said.

"I'm thinking about Tony and Sasha. No way they'd believe that we could be in a motel room for twenty minutes and . . ." He pulled his arm from her and dropped it on his lap.

"And still have our pants on?"

"Exactly."

"So it won't happen tonight?"

"You want to? I always thought . . . you've said . . ."

"A minute ago I wanted to. It passed. It's okay, Mac. It's smart."

"Cory, don't get me wrong. There have been lots of times when I feel like I want to. Ten minutes ago, when you were wiping off the blood, I felt it. And most evenings after we say good night, I sure as hell feel like it. Feel like blowing a hole in my pants, to be precise."

"Don't be crude, Mac."

A tangle of angry shouts and sharp laughter rose from the parking lot outside the door. They listened until the voices had moved around to the front of the building.

"I can't risk it, Cory. At this point in my life I can't risk what might happen to you, or us. I want to, believe me, but right now if I let go —"

"It's okay, Mac. Please don't make me feel like I was begging for it."

"Sorry. Mostly, I'm trying to convince myself."

"You convinced me. Now, hush." She shifted until she was holding him, her arm draped around his shoulders, her fingers resting on his arms. She closed her eyes and tipped her head against his. It was good enough.

12

VOICES COLLECTED outside the door, and Cory rose out of a dream.

A lock clicked, and Cory opened her eyes.

Cold air rushed through the doorway, and she sat up.

The light went on, and she looked straight at Mr. Bartleby. "Damn," she whispered.

"What the hell?" he said. "Cory Knutson, what the hell are you doing in this motel room?" He was accompanied by three men. One of them laughed and pointed at the bed.

"That's what she's doing."

Mac sat up and swung his legs off the bed. "Time to go, Cory."

"Good idea, Mac."

Mr. Bartleby was breathing heavily. His entire chest rose and dropped as he collected air to speak. "I bring these gentlemen up here to show them the only room not taken, and I find you here with your boyfriend."

"Are my shoes over there, Mac?"

"Yes. Catch. Do you see my sweatshirt?"

"Right here."

Mr. Bartleby moved into the room. His companions followed, engrossed and smiling. "Did you do this often, Cory? Is that why you would forget the keys, so you could sneak back with this boy?"

"I'm ready, Mac."

"Me too."

"Cory Knutson, I oughta call the sheriff and get you charged with trespassing. I oughta, I oughta do that."

Cory put on her jacket and pulled the key ring out of a pocket. "I really wish I hadn't quit this afternoon, Mr. Bartleby."

"Too late. I won't accept —"

"Because then I could quit now." She let go of the ring and it dropped with a noisy clatter onto his shoe.

Cory was certain a thousand people stood in the parking lot and watched as she and Mac exited the motel, descended the steps, and walked toward the park and her car. Mac counted seven.

They didn't speak until they were in the car. "Was that funny?" Mac said. "I think maybe that was funny. I wish I'd been awake to see his face when the light went on."

Cory started the car. The headlights revealed shadowy figures milling in front of Unit 26. "It wasn't funny at all. I'd like to kill someone. Anyone."

"Maybe I'll walk home."

129

Cory wrenched the stick shift into position and pounded the gas pedal. The car lurched back and the engine died. She restarted the car, shifted smoothly, and made a careful exit from the park.

In Barb's driveway they parked under the spotlight. A curtain moved slightly and then fell back in place. After a moment the spotlight went off.

Cory smiled. "Does that mean they like me?"

"They like you a lot." He reached for her hand. "How long were we asleep?"

Cory checked the digital time display on the dash. "Maybe an hour. It's not that late."

"Would you like to come in?"

"No." She slouched down in the seat. "Oh, man," she said in a low, slow moan.

"You're making animal noises. What's wrong?"

"School will be awful on Monday. Everyone will know Bartleby caught us."

"Caught us doing nothing."

"That won't be part of the story." She kissed his hand. "You are a fun date, Harvey MacNamara."

"Good night, Cory K."

The ringing phone pierced Cory's sleep. She opened her eyes, established her whereabouts, stumbled out of bed, and walked to the hall phone. She covered her eyes to shield them from sunlight streaming in through a curtainless window.

It was Elaine. "Rob's in jail," she said immediately. Cory woke completely and imagined the worst: he had lied about the blanks and had shot someone. "What happened?"

"He's so stupid. Why did I have to love a stupid guy?"

"What happened, Elaine?"

"A few of the protesters, including our favorite hot-head, broke through the rope. When the deputies arrested them and dragged them away, they saw Rob's gun."

"He told me it just had blanks."

"It did, but it's still a concealed weapon. And in Wisconsin, that's a no-no. My dad is down there arranging to get him out. He's actually proud of Rob."

"And you're not, obviously. Poor Rob — the women in his life have deserted him."

"A gun, he thought a gun was a good idea." Cory could hear Elaine pounding on the table. "I do love him, Cory, but I'm so angry."

"Things will cool down. Things will be okay."

"As long as he doesn't have to go to jail for a lifetime."

"I think marriage to Rob would be easier if he were in jail."

"There's something else that makes it a little complicated. I'm pregnant."

"Elaine, that's great! No, it's awful. Rob a dad. Am I awake? Is this a bad dream?"

"Thanks for the support and comfort."

"Does he know?"

"Yes. I made the mistake of telling him just before he

left yesterday. I thought maybe it would cool him off, get him to think things through. It did just the opposite. He was so pumped up when he left for the landing."

"How are you feeling?"

"I've been better. Rob should be a happy guy. He's going to be a father and now he's famous. It's been all over the radio and in the paper."

"Your pregnancy?"

"Very funny. His arrest. He'll like the publicity. Did you see the article in the paper?"

"I just got up."

"It could have been worse, I keep telling myself that. He might have actually shot someone. Wait — I think I hear them pulling into the driveway."

"Tell Rob I say he's stupid, I love him, and to call me. And congratulations on the baby."

Rob didn't call but nearly everyone else did, wanting to know more about his arrest. Cory explained to each that she knew little and didn't know when she would hear more. With each call she hesitated before answering, expecting to be confronted by someone with questions about what happened in Unit 26. She knew it was just a matter of time. Mr. Bartleby had been practice-talking his whole life, she decided, in preparation for a story this good.

Mac called. "How are you doing?"

"Waiting for the world to collapse. Heard about Rob?"

"Yeah. If it were anyone but your brother I wish they'd lock him up for a long time. I'm sorry, Cory. I guess I'm just starting to get angry now."

"How's your cut?"

"Fine. Roxanne came by earlier and checked it out. I don't know if I should tell you this, but she had already heard about us and the motel."

"Damn."

"I had to make a few corrections to her story. We weren't naked, were we?"

"Why did you call and tell me this?"

"To cheer you up. I feel better."

"I don't. Thanks for the warning. I think I'll run away before anyone else calls."

She didn't have a chance. Moments after she said good-bye to him, the phone rang again. And when she heard Karin purr hello, she knew it was too late.

"Hello yourself," she snapped.

"Guess what I heard?"

"I can't imagine."

"I heard that Cory Knutson delivers room service at Bartleby's Inn!"

"Did you call for a reason, Karin?"

"Nick's older sister caught us once and it was awful, but that's nothing like Bartleby walking in."

"You don't know the whole story, okay? So just keep your mouth shut about it."

"Sneaking into a hotel room with stolen keys is pretty low. Doesn't Mac have a tepee pitched some-where in the woods you could use?"

Cory hung up. She grabbed her jacket, left the house, and walked down to the lake. A few skin-thin patches of ice floated on the water. She sat on a large, flat rock that had warmed slightly from the sun and leaned back against a boulder. The rock chair was a favorite spot, sheltered from the sun in summer by a canopy of leafy tree branches. Today the branches were stark spindles against a blue sky. She stretched out her legs. As a little girl she'd come to the rock to play and read and sneak forbidden snacks. Now she needed to think and wait and do a little wishing. "Things will be fine," she said loudly, startling a small bird into flight. "Just fine." Her wish list was short: that Rob wouldn't go to jail again, that Mike would come home, that the motel story would die an early death, and that her mother's soul was somehow resting in peace. "I wish, I wish, I wish," she chanted softly. "I wish none of this were true."

Her short night's rest and the warm sun conspired, and Cory, nestled into the smooth hollows of the gray rock, closed her eyes and slept.

While sucked deep into the nonsensical frenzy of a dream (in which she was being chased down a never-ending water slide by a bare-chested Mr. Bartleby as he waved a bloody pillowcase), she felt a mosquito bite her shoulder and slapped it.

"Ow!"

Cory opened her eyes. Mike was crouched next to her, rubbing his hand. "Hello. I guess that means you're glad to see me."

"I thought you were a mosquito."

"Too early in the season for those."

"I didn't expect you home so soon."

He sat and started patting his pockets in his habitual

search for cigarettes. He had quit smoking when Cory's mother had first come home from the hospital, but his hands often still searched. He finally drew up his knees and hugged them. "I read about Rob in the paper and I wanted to get home. I've already stopped at Elaine's parents' to see him."

"Was he still alive when you left the house?"

"I wasn't rough on him at all. I even apologized for reacting so extremely yesterday, for throwing them out. He has other problems now and doesn't need to be fighting with his stepfather. We've made a tentative peace, Cory."

"Will they be moving back from the Crenshaws'?"

"I've told him they can, but Rob isn't sure he wants to. We're invited over for dinner tonight. We'll eat and talk things through. It's a start. Now tell me about your night. Did you manage to stay out of trouble?"

Cory closed her eyes and imagined she was in a car traveling in a new place. A rocky coastline, or the mountains. She'd never seen an ocean, never seen mountains.

"Cory?"

She opened her eyes and smiled at her stepfather. His concern eased a fraction. "I have to tell you something, Mike. I have to tell you before you hear it someplace else."

He shifted. "That sounds ominous."

"I screwed up a little bit last night and did something I shouldn't have. Mac and I."

"Get to it, Cory. Tell me."

She told him about the mob at the landing and the men who harassed Mac at the café, told him about Mac's cut and the blood. She told him about the strange mix of fear and wonder and anger on Mac's face when he refused to be taken home or to the doctor. She explained why they went to the motel, what they did there, and how they had talked, then listened to the hateful noise and shouting on the street.

"We fell asleep," she said finally. "Bartleby barged in an hour later and thought he found us having sex. Totally innocent."

"You did trespass."

"I know, Mike, but we couldn't really go anywhere else. Not the way he was bleeding."

He patted his pockets absently, then clasped his hands. "You're lucky he didn't call the sheriff. Boy, that would have been great — two of my kids in jail on the same night!" He lowered his head and shook it slowly. "Margaret," he whispered, "I'm sorry. I'm trying, I'm trying my best."

"There is a little good news. About Elaine. But maybe it's not so good. Didn't she tell you?"

"I only saw Rob. What?"

"She's pregnant."

The announcement had a calming effect on Mike. Cory watched as he relaxed. He smiled and nodded slightly several times. "Good," he finally said. "She would have been so happy about that."

"Yes."

"Look." He pointed to a nearby cluster of fresh green

that was pushing through the brown mat of winter ground cover. "Crocus shoots." He hugged her, and Cory closed her eyes to enjoy the strong, steady rock in his arms. "Let's hope the worst has passed, Cory. A baby's coming, and things always get better in spring."

13

"WHO NEEDS a fresh one?" Rob shouted through the kitchen window to where Cory and Elaine were sitting on the deck. "I guessed wrong on the coals and we have time for another round." He appeared at the door, balancing bottles on a small tray. "Where did the others go?"

"Down front," said Elaine as she reached for a soda. "Dad had to show Mike where the new azalea bed will go in." Elaine's parents owned a nursery and garden store. Their front yard, which stretched nearly a quarter mile to the greenhouses along the highway, was an ever-changing showcase for the family business. Cory had always preferred the back yard with its simple cedar deck and small square of ordinary grass.

"I think it's time for you to stop," Cory said to her brother. "I've never seen you go over two beers."

"There's lots you haven't seen me do, Sis."

"Like cook for company. This is a first, and a grilled pork roast, even. I'm impressed, Robbie."

"A pork roast isn't that difficult," he said. "You just rub it down with garlic and toss it on the grill."

"And wait," said Elaine, "and wait and wait and wait. Meanwhile, I will deliver these cold beers down front."

Rob scratched at the label on his beer bottle. Cory knew how much energy was being directed into that single action, as if it were a release valve that kept him from exploding. She reached out to rub his arm and he jumped.

"Cool down, Robbie."

"Sorry."

"It's good news about the baby."

"You think so?"

"Yes I do. Elaine will be a great mom. C'mon, Robbie, a month ago you wanted a baby."

"A month ago I had a job and money coming in."

"You'll be working soon."

He set the bottle on a table. "Fred Strickler came by this afternoon. He said they'd made a decision that they couldn't give me the job until my legal troubles had cleared up. He said they can't hire someone who might be serving time."

"Too bad, Rob."

"I gave up a good job to work at the plant. They promised."

"You hated the road job. And you got yourself in trouble. You didn't have to go to the landing last night."

He turned and his eyes burned into her. "They're giving my job to the next guy on the list, Peter Rosebear's nephew. He doesn't even live in Summer. That was my job and they gave it to someone else. Three years I waited for my name to come up. They gave it to a goddamn Indian." He pounded on the deck rail. "My job, Cory. My job!"

"Stop it, Rob. I don't want to hear it."

"I bet you don't." He blew across the neck of the beer bottle. "Fred's cousin came to town for the protest, and according to Fred he was one of the guys with Brad last night when they found you. What a cheap deal, Cory. My sister caught by my friends stealing into a motel room with her goddamn Indian boyfriend."

"Stop it."

"Bad enough I lose my job to one of them, but to have you sleeping —"

"Is that what's killing you? Not remorse for your stupid actions last night, not concern about maybe going to jail with a baby on the way? But it's the thought of me in bed with Mac!"

Rob rose. Cory stood and faced him. "Are you going to hate me forever just because I did it with an Indian?"

"You fool."

"I did it, Rob. I did it with an Indian!"

Words lashed as his hand swiped. "You slut!"

The force of the strike came in its surprise. Cory toppled backward. The full weight of her falling body

140

landed on her right arm just as it hit the edge of the cedar rail. The rail bent but held. Her forearm cracked. Cory crumpled and cradled her arm. Blood trickled where his ring had cut across her face.

Rob crouched by her. "Oh God, Cory. Oh, Sis, I'm sorry. I don't know why —"

"Go away," she screamed. She lifted her leg to kick him.

That's how the others found them: Rob kneeling in wide-eyed terror and Cory collapsed and bleeding, one leg thrust out. The dinner party was over.

"I hate hospitals," Mike said as he escorted Cory into the emergency room.

"Don't tell them what happened. I don't want anyone knowing anything about Rob hitting me. We've already given people enough to talk about."

Cory went alone to the exam room. She sat with her eyes closed and cradled her arm as the nurse chatted. When the questions began, she answered in muted monosyllables. "I fell," she mumbled. That was true enough, and all anyone needed to know. If she went any further she'd have to tell the whole story or make it up, and she had already told one big, fat lie tonight, one she had aimed as a direct hit at her brother's weakest spot.

I did it with an Indian.

It wasn't the first lie of her life. She'd told them as a child when she hoped to avoid punishment for minor rule-breaking. Lies to her suspicious mother when she faked sickness to gain an extra day for unfinished homework. Lies to friends about their occasional terrible haircuts.

But never before had she lied with the intent of hurting someone.

"I didn't hear you," the nurse said. "How did it happen?"

"I fell," Cory said firmly.

An hour later she walked out of the hospital with several pounds of fiberglass on her right arm. Mike tucked her good arm under his own. "At least it was a simple fracture. You were lucky."

"I don't feel very lucky."

When Mike laughed, Cory marched ahead to the truck. He went after her and attempted a hug, but was rebuffed.

She turned on him as soon as they were together in the truck cab. "I'm seventeen, motherless, the joke of Summer, I was just punched out by my brother, and you think it's all funny! I'm not laughing, Mike. Look at me — I'm not laughing."

Neither was he. "If anyone had told me a few months ago when your mother was dying that things could get worse, I would never have believed it. This is worse, Cory, and I was laughing because it's the only thing I *can* do." He gripped the steering wheel with both hands and stared ahead. "Somebody, please wake me up."

"I've been wishing the same thing."

For the first few miles, Mike fiddled with the radio,

then turned it off in exasperation. No baseball. He hummed a few soft notes and Cory smiled. The Best Song Ever.

"Mom would be so mad, don't you think?"

"Damn right she'd be mad. And I am too. Cory, if I thought Robbie had ever hit anyone before or was likely to do it again, I'd call the sheriff. It's basic: you don't slug women."

"I don't want him arrested. I don't ever want to see him again, but I don't want him arrested."

"I'm sure you feel that way. With time —"

"Ever. Ever. Keep him away. You want to know why? I can't promise I won't hit *him*."

Mike had a white-knuckle grip on the steering wheel, holding on as if he believed only the sheer force of his will would get them safely home. She could tell he was drawn inside, traveling on another personal, anguished journey. Cory wanted to know, but didn't dare ask, what he was thinking. Wanted to know how it felt to be left with his dead wife's warring children. And whether he wished they'd go away. She wondered if he regretted adopting her. She wanted to know why she had never once called him "Dad."

The scene with Rob replayed over and over in her mind. She heard again her taunting lie, his spat reply. *You slut.* She closed her eyes and saw his hand slashing across her face. Saw the trees spin as she fell. Saw herself kicking and screaming, saw Mike's anguished terror. She squeezed her eyes tighter and brought up other pictures. Cory saw her mother's pale face — dead or asleep, she didn't know. She saw Mac's bloody forehead, saw his injured eyes, saw the laughing strangers in the hotel room. Again and again she saw her brother's enraged face, saw his hand slashing down. Cory opened her eyes and looked out on the dark and featureless forest speeding by. She saw a simple truth: the deepest wounds are bloodless.

14

"DID YOU break your arm falling out of a motel bed?" Nick said.

Cory dropped her jacket into the locker. "Get lost."

"You didn't happen to make copies of the keys, did you?" asked Karin. "I'd like to borrow them sometime."

Cory slammed the gray steel door closed. "Why? Tired of doing it in a car parked at the dump?"

Mac's arrival halted Karin's retort. She turned to him. "You look like a happy boy. Have you been getting more exercise lately?"

Cory stepped in front of Karin and jabbed at Karin's chest with her forefinger. "That's it. That's the last crack, Karin. You've had fun with it. Now just shut up." Karin turned on her heels, grabbed Nick by the arm, and walked away.

"And we're not friends anymore," Cory called after her. The corridor was filled with students hurrying to first-hour classes. Cory's shout slowed traffic for a moment. "Hey, people," she called out, "did you hear everything?" The rush resumed.

Mac tapped her cast. "What happened here?"

"I fell. I fell, I fell, I fell. End of story."

Sasha slipped out of the crowd and dropped her bag and jacket on the floor. "I slept late. I didn't sleep at all Saturday and so I crashed for twelve hours last night. I didn't hear my alarm go off and my stupid stepmother couldn't take her eyes off Donahue long enough to wake me up. Hi, you guys. Have you seen Tony? This lock never works. Finally." She exchanged books, stashed her jacket, and slammed the locker closed. "What an incredible weekend. My God, Cory, what did you do to your arm?"

"She fell," said Mac. "End of story. And Tony's already in class. He had to talk to Señor Burger about a test." He kissed Cory on the top of her head. "It hasn't been too bad. Only three or four people have said anything. Don't let them get to you, okay? Catch you later, Sash." Mac stepped into the flow and was swept toward his classroom.

"What's he talking about?" Sasha asked.

Cory leaned against the lockers. "You haven't heard?"

The warning bell rang. "I haven't heard anything. I spent all day yesterday with some people from Milwaukee who came up to be witnesses. What should I have heard?"

Cory told her about why and how they had been discovered in the motel room, and even before she was

146

finished Sasha let out a gleeful howl. "No! Bartleby? I bet he hasn't climbed steps in ten years. That is hilarious."

"No, it's not."

"Yes, it is. You'll laugh someday. It's great. Does Mike know?"

"I told him. He was a little upset because I trespassed. He feels like he failed my mother, what with both kids screwing things up."

The final bell rang and they were alone in the halls. "I saw Rob get arrested," Sasha said.

"I don't want to hear about it. I am so mad at him. If we hurry we won't need a tardy slip." They jogged down the hall, book bags bouncing against their hips.

"How did you hurt your arm?"

"I fell."

"Fell how? Climbing mountains? Washing windows? Getting out of the tub?" When they reached their class, Sasha looked in and noted the absence of a teacher and the student mayhem. "We have a minute. How did you fall?"

Cory spotted their teacher at the far end of the hall. "Don't tell. You have to promise not to tell."

"You've got it. How?"

"My brother hit me and I fell."

"On purpose?"

"No, I didn't fall on purpose. Here comes Steadman. Let's go."

"Wait. He hit you on purpose?"

"Shush. Yes. We were arguing and . . . hi, Mr. Steadman. We'll be right in."

"Class starts now, girls." He waited for them to enter, then followed and closed the door.

Cory and Sasha took their seats. Sasha leaned over as she fished a pencil out of her bag. "Want me to kill him for you?"

"Not anymore," Cory whispered. "But if you had offered last night —"

"Cory and Sasha, you may finish your conversation later." Mr. Steadman turned his back and began listing dates on the board. "A short quiz, students. Please put away your textbooks and take out pencil and paper."

Sasha spoke under the cover of the noise of ripping paper and murmured complaints. "What did Mac say?"

"I didn't tell him."

"I think you should —"

"Sasha and Cory, if you must talk you may do it in the principal's office. For those who are paying attention, here are your quiz instructions."

Cory was trying to remember the historical significance of 1619 when Sasha slid a note onto her desk. Keeping an eye on the teacher, she unfolded it slowly: "What will you do about your brother? Press charges?"

She smoothed the paper and scribbled a reply: "Nothing. But I will never — repeat, never — talk to him again."

Cory was surprised by how easy it was to avoid her brother. Even in a town only big enough for two grocery stores it was possible not to cross paths. Rob went his way, she went hers. They nearly met one Friday night at the video section in Zanker's service station. She and Mac were looking through Mystery and Rob was one aisle over in Comedy. She recognized the top of his head. "Pick anything," she whispered to Mac. "I'll wait in the car."

She watched, then couldn't watch, as Mac and Rob met at the register. Instead, she closed her eyes and counted.

"Did he say anything?" she asked as soon as Mac got into the car.

"Who?"

"Rob. What did he say?"

"Not much. He did look at my movie and said you wouldn't like it."

Cory took the plastic box from his lap and opened it. "Mac, I hate subtitles."

"That's what he said. This is supposed to be good, though. You said I could pick anything. Why didn't you want to talk to him?"

"I told you we had a fight."

"My brother and I fought all the time, but we still talked."

"Well, you're perfect."

It was the wrong response and it chilled the evening. After that they didn't speak much, couldn't agree on pizza toppings, and back at Cory's house they were quiet and didn't respond to Mike's jokes. He appraised their moods and retreated to his own room and television with his share of the pizza.

Neither of them enjoyed the movie. When the main character, an unhappy boy, began barking like a dog, Cory punched the off button on the remote control. The VCR whirred and halted. The screen darkened.

"Sorry, Mac. I just wasn't into it."

"Neither was I. I didn't know it was about a kid whose mom died."

Cory sat erect on the sofa, knocking off the pillows she had collected on her lap during the movie. "I liked the title, though. *My Life as a Dog*. It would be a good title for my life."

Mac swore softly, then picked up a pillow and banged it against Cory's knees. "Knock it off, Cory. You're not the only one who's got problems. It really burns me that you're having this fight with your brother and you act like it's the worst thing that has ever happened to anyone. It must have been one hell of a fight."

She yanked the pillow from him. "He hit me. I said something that made him mad and he slapped me. That's when I fell and broke my arm."

She had expected Mac would be angry. That he'd fill up with memories of his mother's battles and wounds and lash out.

Mac nodded and smiled. "That explains a lot."

"Like what?"

He shrugged. "The expression on his face when he asked me to tell you to call him. It explains your anger."

"I thought you'd be mad. I thought you'd . . ."

He scratched at a spot of dried pizza sauce on his

150

jeans. "Remember my mother and get mad at Roger again?"

Exactly. "Something like that."

Mac stretched out and stacked his feet. "Don't be mad forever, Cory. It eats away inside and sometimes makes you crazy. Take my word for it." He reclaimed the pillow, laid it on his lap, and drummed on it with his fingertips. "I've learned two new songs from Jeff. He's so good."

"Why are you changing the subject?"

"*I* want to tell *you* something. Could we possibly talk about my life?"

"Go ahead."

"Barb and Jeff are sending me to Canada this summer. I have to come up with part of the money, but they're paying most of it."

"Canada?"

"I'll visit the reserves where my parents were born. I'll get to meet relatives and maybe go to a program to learn Cree."

"How long will you be gone?"

"Eight or nine weeks."

"Nine weeks? That's most of the summer. How long have you been planning this?"

"That sounds like an accusation. Barb just mentioned it the other day. And it depends a lot on if I can save money and come up with my share. Jeff is hiring me to work with his crew putting in docks and getting summer cabins ready before the season. That will help."

"But you're saving for college, Mac. You'll use up all that money."

"The aid package from the U should cover school. I want to go, Cory. It's something you couldn't possibly understand."

"If Sasha spends the summer with her mother I'm going to be absolutely alone. Mac, couldn't you go whoop it up at Indian camp somewhere around here?"

As soon as it was out she regretted it. His response was measured — a slight shift, a stiffening, but she knew without a doubt that her comment had hit and taken hold. A few quick words, another bloodless wound.

She faced him. "I'm sorry, Mac." It was a heartfelt, pleading apology, but worthless unless it found a welcome.

He nodded. "It's okay. Sometimes you just say things. I've learned that much." He rose and walked to the window. "I really want to go."

"I know you do. And I really don't want you to. Meeting you was the one good thing about this year, and now you're telling me I'm going to lose you, too."

"You're not losing me. I'm not asking to break up or anything. I'm just spending my summer elsewhere."

"I don't see the difference." *Why go now, why now?* she stopped herself from screaming. "Why are you doing this?" she whispered.

"My whole life I've drifted along, going where my mother or Tom took me. And now I've lived a few months in one place, in a good home, with good people. But I feel like any moment I could be picked up and blown away. I've been thinking about this ever since your mother died. Nothing could have stopped it from happening, Cory. No medicine, no doctors. It was her time. But my mother. . . Cory, I really believe if she had stayed with her people, she'd be alive. If she'd had something to hold on to, she wouldn't have had to keep running. I want to be sure I have it, Cory. And maybe I'm just claiming it for her."

A log split and crashed in the fireplace, and sparks flew. A chunk rolled onto the hearth. Mac walked to the fireplace and kicked it back in. He raised his arms above his head and stretched, then pointed across the room. "You still have the dream catcher."

"We wouldn't throw it out."

"I didn't mean that, but you still have it in the same place."

"Mike has kept a lot of her things in the same place. Makeup and perfume on the dresser, clothes in the closet."

"That seems weird."

"It's nice, actually. Nice to have things the way they were."

He sat back down, took her hand, and stared into her eyes. He was never without something to say, but this once he seemed unable to bring it up. She waited, staring back, willing him to say what he was thinking.

"I've got to go," he said finally.

After they said good night, she returned to the living room and turned off the lights. She sat still and listened to his car start and drive away. Cory put a log on the fire and lay on the floor, her head resting on stacked fists. She heard Mike moving about in his room, then it was quiet. Out of the corner of her eye, she saw the golden glint of the dream catcher. She rose, dragged a chair to the corner, climbed on it, and lifted the web off the hook. Mac hadn't needed to say a word; she understood his unspoken message. Things weren't the way they were. Everything had changed.

15

CORY AND Mike were eating breakfast the next morning when they heard a car pull into the driveway. Mike rose and carried his empty coffee mug to the sink and looked out the window. "Company for you. I'll be outside splitting wood."

Cory checked the clock. Nine A.M. Too early for Sasha, and Mac always called first. She smiled and sipped cocoa. Maybe Bartleby had driven out to offer her a job. Then Rob walked into the kitchen. Without speaking he poured himself coffee, pulled a chair from the table, and sat down.

Cory had choices. She could leave and walk down to the lake, but she would be cold in her pajamas. She could go to her bedroom, but Rob had blocked — not by accident, she was certain — the route to her room and she'd have to ask him to move. Or she could throw tableware and newspaper at him until he left. She poked at her cold oatmeal with a spoon until she had made a pale beige mound. Oatmeal would look good in his hair.

"I need to talk with you. I don't want you to avoid me any longer. I'm sorry, Cory. I am so incredibly, deeply sorry. I hit my sister and I've been really sick about it. And God damn you for not letting me say I'm sorry."

He waited for her response. She gave none but didn't leave or move, and that was all the encouragement he needed.

"Reasons aren't excuses, but I know why it happened. Have you ever had a day when everything you touch goes bad, everything you do goes wrong? That was one helluva day: I'd been arrested, spent the night in jail, screwed things up with my wife, lost my chance at a good job. It was all just closing in on me, Cory. Then you started shouting at me and I wanted it all to stop. Just stop. Everything."

"So you hit me."

"Hit you and hated you. Double whammy. I'm sorry, Cory."

Neither of them spoke, and the silence went on and on until Rob sipped coffee and slurped loudly.

Cory laughed. "Mom always hated your table manners. She had a point."

"Mostly I did stuff just to bug her. She was so easy to get going sometimes. Remember?"

"I remember."

"Look, Cory, I'm not here just to apologize. Elaine and I have rented our own place. I've started working for her folks. I'm supervising the landscaping crew."

Cory had already heard. She hadn't talked to her brother for three weeks, but she had heard plenty about him. Heard he was working for his in-laws, heard his criminal charges had been reduced to misdemeanors, heard when Elaine had an appointment with the obstetrician in Wausau.

"We have this new place and next week we're throwing a party. Sort of a housewarming, but mostly a birthday party for Mike. He'll be fifty."

Cory covered her face with her hands and groaned. She'd forgotten.

"He deserves a great party, one with all his friends and all his family. I want to give it to him, and I want you to come." He took a deep breath, clasped his hands and slid them between his legs. "Bring Mac."

Last night Mac had let her say she was sorry. He had taken the punch of her flip remark about Indian camp, let her breathe in and out, let her apologize. He could have left, could have decided she'd shown true, racist feelings. Could have decided it was all over. But he had let her apologize.

Cory smashed the oatmeal mountain. "It's okay, Robbie. I made an easy target for you."

He needed a moment to understand that she had shifted to the original subject. "Oh. Well. The blame is mine. I hit."

"I lied. I wanted to hurt you, I wanted to hurt you so bad." She was close to crying. She could feel some internal vise twist her face, could feel the tears squeeze

157

toward the surface. "The party is a great idea. We'll be there."

"I hope *he* thinks it's a great idea. It's a surprise party."

"Fifty. Mom used to threaten him with a big party."

"I know. 'A blowout when you're fifty, old man,' she'd say. She's gone, so I figured we'd better carry on. I don't know if we can really keep it a surprise because I'm inviting everyone. His kids, the guys from the plant, Mom's friends from work —"

"Peter?"

"He's coming."

"And Roxanne? To your house?"

"I said everyone. Don't push it, Cory."

"Excuse me for being surprised, Robbie, but three weeks ago you would have shot an Indian on sight." She raised her arm. "You broke my arm, remember? Do you remember what this is all about? You hit me." She shook her head slowly. "You can't convince me everything's different. A party doesn't change things."

"I'm trying to change, okay? It's slow, but I'm trying."

"You're a new man?"

"Don't get sarcastic. Don't get flip and sarcastic. No, I'm not a new man. I still think the same things, I still feel the same. When I think about how they can have special rights in a place that's my home, too, I burn up and want to explode."

"So you throw a party. Logical."

158

"For Mike. And I'm smart enough to want things to be different. For chrissake, Cory, our mother is dead, and I've got a baby on the way who won't ever know her. That hurts. And when I hit you I came pretty damn close to making sure the baby would never know you or Mike. I won't let that happen. I won't." He looked toward the window and seemed to direct his words to the outside, or the world beyond. "I'll do anything," he whispered.

His emotion charged her. She dug her fingernails into her palm. She wasn't sure what he expected, wasn't sure what he needed. Wasn't even sure what she felt inside.

"Anything?"

A slight nod.

"Pierce your ear?"

His tension — and hers — released in a nearly audible hiss. Rob smiled. "I have my limits. I've got to go. We're putting down two lawns today." He rose, leaned down, and kissed her. "Is everything okay, then?"

Cory pushed back. "No, Rob, everything's not okay. It doesn't get fixed that easily. Better, maybe. Just better." Cory rose and carried her dishes to the sink.

"Nice pajamas. I like the way you mix a striped shirt with plaid pants. That shirt, by the way, is mine. I bought it in New Orleans on my senior trip."

"You left it here." The dream catcher lay on the counter. She had known last night that it needed to come down but had been uncertain about where to put it. Drops of water that had splashed from the sink glistened on the gold filament. Cory slipped her little finger through the loop of string and lifted the web. "Why don't you take this and put it in the baby's room? Unless you don't want anything Indian in your house." She bit her lip. Words slipped out so easily.

Rob walked around the table. "Do you think Mike will mind?"

"I think he'll like it that I gave it to you."

Rob slipped it into his jacket pocket. "I'll put it over the crib. Keeps away bad dreams, isn't that it?"

"No nightmares allowed."

"Thanks, Sis. This means a lot."

He hugged her, holding on until her stiffness dissolved and she raised her arms and was holding him. Then Cory stepped back. "You said you had to get to work."

"Are we friends again?"

"Brother and sister. Friends, we'll work on."

"Good enough. And your brother would like to ask a favor."

"What?" She dragged the word into two syllables.

"Don't be so suspicious. Could you come early on Friday and help set up things before the party? Bring Mac."

"I can do that."

"And one more thing. I'd like —"

Enough. Not even ten in the morning and she had already overloaded the day with emotions and memories. Enough.

"What, Robbie?" she snapped. "I've forgiven you. I've hugged you. I gave your baby a precious gift. What more do you want?"

"Ease up. It's okay." He pointed at her. "I just want my shirt back."

16

NEARLY EIGHTY people were crowded into Rob and Elaine's tiny house waiting to surprise Mike. Cory had come to the house directly after school to help with preparations. Once the first guests arrived she called Mike to report car trouble and ask for a ride home. When his car was spotted turning onto the street, Rob gave a signal that triggered an increase in the chatter and laughter as everyone tried to squeeze into the living room to hide. Cory and Mac were jammed together against a wall near the front door. Tony's dad was crushed against them.

Cory mustered a smile. Face to face with the town's number-one bigot. The last time she had seen him he had been leaning over the restraining rope at the landing, so steeped in venom he nearly drooled.

"Some party," he said.

"He's out of the car!" someone shouted.

"Be careful, Mac," Jack Merrill said. "If you try to

162

hold Cory's hand in this crowd you might discover you made a move on a strange woman."

Peter Rosebear twisted around from his position behind a coatrack. "Too bad nobody warned Sally Webber, Jack. She was headed to the kitchen and she thought she was next to her husband —"

"Hush!" Elaine called. "He's coming up the steps."

Peter tipped his head and whispered his story to Tony's father. When he finished the two men lit up and shook with silent, suppressed glee.

Cory watched, amazed. The two men giggling over some mildly lewd party story appeared to be the best of friends. It was as if the two of them had never been on opposite sides at the landing.

Rob inched through the crowd toward the front door. He tapped Mac on the shoulder and produced one of his thousand-watt, life-is-great smiles. "I hope the roof stays on when this crowd yells surprise."

"Good party, Robbie," said Mac.

Cory tapped her cast and stroked the rough, nearly healed line on her cheek. Reality check.

The roof did stay on when the crowd bellowed a greeting. Mike stood still and shook his head. Then Cory broke forward and pulled him in, and the party roared to life.

Cory danced with every middle-aged man at the party, except Mr. Bartleby. She just wouldn't talk to the man; the protesters and the spearers could pretend nothing had ever happened, but she had her standards.

When Tony's dad motioned her toward the small space in the living room that had been claimed by dancers, she realized she'd had enough. She shook her head, then fought her way to the back of the house. Mike was in the hallway outside the two bedrooms talking with three coworkers from the factory. He hauled her into a hug.

"Thanks for the party."

"Rob's idea."

"But you came."

Mike's daughter appeared behind some people. She lifted her baby up and passed it over someone's shoulder. "Be a good grandpa," she said to Mike, "and change her diaper. Rob has a crib set up, and she might go down for a nap."

Mike offered the baby to Cory. She took a step backward. "When was the last time you changed a diaper?"

She didn't want to say.

Mike cradled the infant in his arm. "Have you ever changed a diaper?"

"Is that a crime? I was never into baby-sitting."

Mike whistled. "Time for a lesson, Aunt Cory."

Elaine wasn't due for nearly six months, but she and Rob had already begun preparing a nursery in the smallest bedroom. They had repaired an old changing table and crib, and hung posters and mobiles. A picture of Cory's mother was framed and propped on a shelf adjacent to the changing table. The dream catcher hung over the crib. Suspended from a ceiling hook on a clear thread of fishing line, it swayed with the vibrations of the party.

Cory listened absently as Mike gave diapering instructions. They both stood by the crib as he laid his granddaughter down. The baby flopped her head twice on the mattress, sucked her thumb into her mouth, and closed her eyes.

Mike tapped the dream catcher. "It was a nice idea to give this to Rob."

"It didn't seem right to keep it where it was, not forever."

"No."

Someone squealed in the hallway, which triggered an increase in the noise.

"What do you suppose...?" Mike wondered.

Cory shook her head. "Some party, old man."

"Have you danced with Brad Bartleby yet? He may not look it, but he's a good dancer."

"No way. Never." Her voice rose as her protest increased. "Not for —"

"Shush. Baby's stirring." Mike pulled a blanket over the small, sleeping body.

Someone knocked on the door, and then a head popped in. "This the bathroom?"

"Next to the kitchen," Mike whispered. The door closed.

"It's all a mystery to me," Cory said.

"Finding a bathroom? I guess you haven't been to many wild parties in your life. That's good."

"I mean it's a mystery how all these people can have such a good time together." She pointed at the door. "Like that guy. He was at the landing, but twenty minutes ago he was dancing with Roxanne like they were old high school sweethearts. You've got a house

165

full of the town's worst bigots acting like they're best friends with every Indian they've ever known. I don't get it. Are they just going to pretend the landing never happened? Was Rob's gun just a joke? Was the cut on Mac's head an accident?" She thumped her cast. "I know my brother hit me."

"Would you rather no one got along, even for a night?"

"Of course not. But if they just pretend nothing happened, nothing will ever change."

"Things will change. Maybe just one person, one heart —"

"I've heard it, Mike. It's sickening and idealistic."

He shook his head vigorously. "I thought so, too, when Margaret used to lay it on me. One at a time, she'd say. Usually after one of the nursing home residents quit complaining about having Rox or one of the other Indian nurses and stopped demanding a white nurse. One at a time. Your mother convinced me that it's actually a pessimistic view because it means believing that there is no other way things will get better."

"I don't think anyone has changed. They just wanted to come to a party, so they buried their feelings for one night."

Mike tugged on her arm and pulled her toward the door. "It's not that hopeless. Robbie's changed a little. He's seen and felt the consequences of his hate, Cory, and I think it's made a difference. The others," he said, shrugging, "well, maybe one or two or a few will have buried their feelings so deep they can't be dug up." He switched on a night-light and turned off the large lamp. "The birthday boy should return to the party. By the way, I explained things to Brad, about Mac's cut and why you were in the motel room. He said you could have come to the office. He said he would have helped."

"I don't believe that for a moment."

"Maybe not. But he believes it. That's something." Mike kissed her. "Enjoy the party, sweetheart."

Cory watched the revelers from the hallway. She couldn't believe that a magic wand had brushed the town and healed it. She knew that next spring when spearing began, there would be protests again. Loud and angry.

Laughter erupted and she focused her attention. Roxanne was concluding a story that had convulsed her listeners. Then another woman in the group — a clerk at the IGA who had been a protester — began talking and the other women quieted and leaned forward eagerly, hands on shoulders, heads tipped together.

There would be protests, Cory decided. But possibly Mike was right and there would be one or two fewer screamers at the ropes.

Maybe her mother's revolution would happen. One party at a time.

"Snap out of it, Cory. I have to talk with you. Now." Sasha stepped out of the crowd, grabbed her arm, and pulled her toward the nursery.

"There's a baby sleeping."

"Doesn't matter as long as you don't scream."

They slipped into the darkened room and closed the door.

"What's up?"

"You will not believe what I found out. But it makes so much sense. Why didn't we guess?"

"Tell me."

"I was standing in line for the bathroom. They really should have a second bathroom; I almost died."

"Sasha."

"I was waiting in the hall. Right around the corner in the kitchen Nick's dad was talking to Logan Bennett's dad, okay? And Mr. Bennett was telling how last winter he went to Logan's room to borrow a sweatshirt. So he opened a drawer, he says, and found five boxes of the things."

"The things?"

"Condoms. And they were all the same brand: Mighty Max, multicolored."

"It could be a coincidence."

"Five boxes of the same brand? But that's not all. Mr. Bennett said he went back two days later and they were gone. Gone! In your locker, that's where they were. Then Nick's dad said something crude and then it was time for the bathroom."

"I hardly know Logan. Why would he do all that stuff?"

"His ego. Logan asks you out, you say no, then you start going out with Mac. It's so obvious, Cory. On Monday we tell Donaldson."

"No."

"You have to! This guy has been harassing you. Racist, sexist harassment."

"No."

"I'm going to scream, Cory! You're driving me crazy and I'm going to scream."

"Settle down."

"You have to do something."

"I will."

"What?"

Cory leaned against the wall. The night-light cast a yellow beam that reflected off the glass over her mother's picture. Cory turned back to Sasha. Her mother's eyes hadn't really been burning, it was a light trick, that's all.

"Have Tony check it out without giving anything away. Guys talk in the locker room. He can find out if he asks the right questions. I want to know for sure."

"And then?"

Cory twisted and looked again at the picture. Eyes glowed in the center of a framed shadow. She turned her back. "I'm going to give Logan a little present."

"Cory?"

"Don't panic, Sasha. I only want to give them back."

17

THE SUMMER HIGH boys' baseball team had an early morning practice before school each weekday. Wind sprints, push-ups, laps around the track, skill drills. Logan Bennett was the starting first baseman on the team, a defensive star with a mediocre batting average.

Cory flattened herself on the asphalt. A tiny piece of gravel bit into her cheek. She pillowed her head with her arm. It was an uncomfortable position, but she didn't dare shift, didn't dare sit up. She couldn't see the team running final laps, but she could hear the coach shouting and could hear the steps on the track.

"That'll do it." Coach Nordquist called. "Showers."

Cory's foot twitched and tapped a soda can. It rolled noisily and banged against a few other cans. Way too much trash. She'd have to get the council to do something about it. Maybe another school cleanup day.

I'm innocent, she thought. I've never tossed anything up here.

She was lying on the roof of a walkway that connected the school's main building to the auditorium and gymnasium. Twelve feet down and several yards away, Sasha was sitting on a bench.

Cory swept her arm out until her fingers touched the straps of her two old book bags. She hadn't used them for years, but now they were heavy and loaded.

She could hear the team running toward her. Closer yet, and she could smell the moist, tangy odor of sweaty guys. She blocked out the conversations, listening intently for Sasha's voice.

The wide doors below her were pulled open and her post shook as the boys hustled through — twenty-five thundering, sweaty animals.

"Logan!" Sasha's sharp call startled even Cory, who had been waiting for it for twenty minutes. "Wait a second, would you?"

Would he stop? Walk away? Was someone with him? Cory didn't dare lift her head to see. She counted the seconds, one...two...three.

"I'm sorry," Sasha said. "Never mind."

Never mind. The all clear. Cory rose to her knees and hauled up a bag. She looked down. Sasha was walking away, and Logan, hands on his hips, stood alone just outside the corridor watching her.

Cory lifted the first bag, tipped it upside-down and shook. The gelatinous, loaded condoms tumbled out and fell.

Logan screamed. Logan swore.

Cory emptied the other bag.

He was still screaming, still swearing.

Cory checked her bags. Two condoms had broken, and there was a gooey mix of ketchup and vegetable oil coating the bottom of one of the bags.

Logan's teammates had returned when he'd started screaming. One of them gingerly toed an unbroken, bloated condom. He nudged it into the grass. It split open and water wet his foot.

"It's Cory Knutson up there!" someone shouted, and Cory waved to the team. Logan looked up. His blond hair was coated with brown. Cory wondered if regular shampoo would get rid of molasses.

Logan pointed and swore. He called her a name.

Cory smiled. "Gotcha."

"She did what?" Mike gasped and gripped his chair. He looked at Cory, looked at Mr. Donaldson, then slumped.

"As I said, she assaulted another student on the school grounds. I appreciate your leaving work and coming down."

"She couldn't assault a rabbit and do any harm."

"She was . . ." Mr. Donaldson chewed on his lower lip and patted the edges of a neat stack of papers. "She was armed."

"Condoms," Cory said. "I filled them. Most of them just had water, but a few had other stuff. And I dropped them on Logan Bennett."

Noise from the outer office filtered in. Cory heard a secretary making announcements over the P.A. She heard a vaguely familiar voice ask to use the phone, heard the more distant chatter and laughter of a class leaving on a field trip.

Mike drummed on his chair arm. "Cory," he whispered, "did you have a reason?"

"It hardly matters," said the principal. "She assaulted Logan and I must take disciplinary action. The, uh, weapon was not dangerous, so I am limiting the suspension to three days. And she will be banned from all extracurricular activities for the remainder of the year."

Cory ran a calendar check: council convention in Madison, spring play, concerts, prom. The tiniest twinge of regret twisted deep inside.

"It does matter if she had a reason," Mike said. "It matters to me. Cory?"

She reached into her pocket. She had been prepared to make a defense and had brought the evidence. She unfolded the two notes and laid them on the principal's desk. "Someone left these in my locker last winter. There was one more, but Sasha got mad and ripped it up. Last weekend I found out it was Logan who wrote them."

After the men read the messages, Mr. Donaldson smoothed them flat, then slipped them into a manila folder. Cory couldn't see if her name was on it.

"These are terrible, of course —"

"Along with the note about diseases, he put a bunch of condoms in my locker. Slipped them through the vents, I guess, because he didn't have my combination. I hardly know the guy. That's why I did it. I was just returning the gift."

She watched for a smile. Watched to see if the absurdity, the silliness, would crack through their stern demeanors. Ketchup and oil and molasses and water. That's all, guys. That's all.

Mike's fist slammed on the desk, then he pulled it back and shoved it into his coat pocket. "What," he said to the principal, "will you do to the boy? Have you investigated this? It's your school, and these notes, this sort of thing, shouldn't be allowed. I cannot support the suspension if you don't do something about the boy. I'll send her to Florida to visit my mother. I'll let her go someplace and have a good time."

"I didn't know a thing about the notes until now. I had no idea."

Mike turned to Cory. "When did this happen? Why didn't you tell me?"

The principal had a nice view out his window. Daffodils and crocuses spread across the lawn. Farther down, there was a dark cluster of trees sheltering a pile of silver, ice-crusted snow. Cory looked at Mike. "Mom was dying."

Mr. Donaldson rose. "Mike, I promise to look into Logan's part in this. If it bears out, I'll certainly take action."

Mike faced him and they shook hands. "Thanks, Ken."

Mr. Donaldson walked around his desk. "I understand Sasha was involved."

"It was my stunt. It's my problem."

"I won't be suspending her, but she, too, will be banned from activities."

Cory closed her eyes and pictured the prom dress in Sasha's closet. She stepped directly in front of the principal. "You can't do that. That's ridiculous. She didn't —"

Her protest was squelched by Mike's sudden grip on her arm. "Let's go," he said. "Before it gets worse."

Sasha was waiting with her stepmother in the outer office. She raised her eyebrows in question. Cory made a slash across her neck.

"That bad?" said Sasha.

"Call me tonight."

Mike paused in the hallway to button his coat. "Three days. You can work on your math."

"I thought I was going to Florida."

"Only if he ignored Logan. Not now. Ken will do what's right."

"I can sleep late, at least."

"You can do your math. This might be your last chance to avoid summer school, Cory."

"I'll watch some soaps."

"This isn't going to be a vacation. Not for a moment. You have been suspended and I'm not happy about it, Cory. Do you understand that?"

"I hear you, Mike."

"I have to go back to work. Can I trust you to get your books and go straight home and study?"

"Of course you can trust me. Have I ever let you down?"

"Dawn's store, algebra, first communion."

"Communion hardly counts."

"You were fourteen, Cory. Old enough to know better than to spit out the wine and blurt 'Yuck.' "

"It gave you a reason to stop going to church, didn't it?"

He didn't answer, didn't seem to have heard. He rubbed his unshaven jaw. "Loaded condoms. Oh, Lord, Cory, your mother —"

"Please don't haunt me with that, Mike. Donaldson's given me plenty of punishment."

He pushed open the exterior door, and a gust of wind blew in their faces. Mike shook his head. "That's not what I was going to say. Once upon a time, given the same situation, your mother would have done exactly the same thing."

"You think so?"

Mike smiled. "Maybe without the molasses."

"But that was the best. It just oozed across the bastard's head. I nearly —"

Mike shushed her with a finger to her lips. "Go home, sweetheart. Go home and study."

18

PROM NIGHT was rainy and cold. Cory picked up Mac, Sasha, and Tony, and for twenty minutes they sat in her car and debated about where to eat dinner. Tony made the final winning point that going to the powwow in Eagle River was Sasha and Mac's idea, so he and Cory should choose the food. Burgers and malts won out over pizza. After dinner at Seestadt's Café, the four friends drove to the school and cruised the parking lot, shouting and honking at formally dressed classmates who were huddling under umbrellas and scurrying through the rain and around puddles toward the gymnasium door.

Cory switched the wipers to high speed. "It's really pouring now. Look — there are Nick and Karin. If I time this just right, I can hit that puddle and splash them."

Sasha cheered her on, Tony sank out of sight, Mac gently squeezed her arm. "Don't you dare."

Cory glanced at Sasha in the rearview mirror. They both rolled their eyes. "The next time I fall in love," Cory announced to her companions, "it will be with someone lacking a conscience."

"What did you say?" Mac asked.

"You have a conscience, Harvey MacNamara. It's not always attractive."

"No — the 'fall in love' part. Did I hear right? Can there be a 'next time' without a 'this time'?"

"Let's hit the highway," said Cory.

"She loves him," Sasha said to Tony. "I always knew it."

Tony pushed against the front seat with his foot. "Tell him straight out, Cory. Guys like it."

"It won't hurt," added Sasha.

"Who wants to walk to Eagle River?" Cory asked. She reached across to Mac and tapped his glasses. "If you're dancing tonight you should take those off."

"I'm not dancing, and you changed the subject."

"It's a private subject, okay? Hey, everyone, it's private."

Sasha and Tony hissed and booed. Mac nodded. "Fair enough."

"How about this, though," she said. "One thing I love about you" — and she reached and slipped a hand into the largest of two rips in his jeans — "is the way you dress. Those purple boxer shorts are great."

Tony leaned over the front seat. "Wow, she has her hand in his pants! Smooth move, Cory."

Sasha yanked him back. "Buckle up."

"Sasha," sighed Tony, "if I rip my jeans, will you

do what Cory did?" Sasha punched him, Mac laughed, Cory accelerated the engine, and they sped toward Eagle River.

As soon as they were in the community center, Sasha spotted the vendors and dragged Tony off to go shopping. Mac led Cory by hand through the crowd. "I guess we're too late for the grand entry," he said. "They've already started the competitions."

Cory stood on tiptoe in order to see into the center of the hall where the dancing was going on. She occasionally saw a headdress rise, then fall out of sight. As they pushed closer to the dancing, Mac was accosted by an excited girl who wanted to talk about someone Cory didn't know, some crazy fool named Don and what he did, what he said. Mac laughed and they talked, heads bowed together. The girl was in a jingle dress of deep red cotton covered with rows of chimes. Tobacco-can lids. As Cory watched them talk, the initial twinge of jealousy gave way to curiosity about Mac's life. Who else, what else, was unknown to her?

She'd always been aware of the imbalance in their lives, always known that his was more complicated, with wider and wilder experience. Hers had always been safely circumscribed by a comfortable life in Summer. And if he went through with his plans for Canada, the disparity would increase. She, after all, was only going to summer school.

"Damn algebra," she said aloud. Her words were lost in the crowd noise. She repeated it again and again, louder each time.

Mac turned around. "What are you saying? Gosh, I'm sorry, Cory. I didn't introduce you. This is Lisa Whitebird. Lisa, this is Cory Knutson."

The jingles on Lisa's dress tinkled as she reached for and shook Cory's hand. "Nice to meet you."

Cory exchanged a few words about the weather, the crowd, the dancing, the noise. She rubbed Mac's arm gently. "Stay and talk, Mac. I'll just push on and look around."

"I'll meet you later by Jeff and his drum group."

"I can find it." She edged through people toward the vendors' tables, hoping to find Sasha and Tony. She circled the hall once, didn't see them, and decided to find Mac, even if she had to drag him away from the girl. She looked around, looked up, and spotted a video camera suspended from the ceiling. It moved slowly from side to side as it recorded. She wondered how she would appear on the tape, what she would look like: one very short white girl pushing her way alone through a mass of feathers, shawls, beads, and jingles.

She saw Mac standing behind Jeff at the drum circle and she found an empty chair. She was close enough to the center to see the dancing. The announcer, whom she couldn't see, said something, people applauded, and the drummers began their song.

The rising and falling voices and the incessant drumming was immediately mesmerizing. She closed her eyes and was carried back to the first powwow, the first time she'd heard the drum, before . . . before everything.

What have I passed on to you?

Cory opened her eyes.

It's important to pass things on. What have I taught you?

Cory had never believed in ghosts, but now, amidst the swirl of drum and song, she heard her mother's voice. It was a forceful haunting of memory and desire.

She rose, looked wildly for an escape, then saw Mac listening to the drum. Focused, intent, unsmiling; still, his pleasure was evident. His eyes were closed, his lips moved, and his hand twitched up and down. She guessed he was silently singing along, committing the song to memory.

Something to hold onto, he had said. His mother hadn't had it, and he was claiming it for her.

Mac looked, saw her, and waved. Cory smiled and sat down. Maybe it wasn't just music running through his mind. Maybe he heard a voice too, his own haunting.

Hers returned, insistent and clear through the loud drumming. *What have I taught you?* Cory glanced down. White shirt, beige bra. "Taught me how to dress," she whispered. "I learned that."

And more, of course. Cory caressed the smooth, pale skin of her once-broken arm. She had also learned something about change, something about revolutions of the heart.

Between songs and dances the chair next to hers emptied and Mac appeared and sat down. "I'm sorry I deserted you."

"Forgiven."

181

"Having a good time?"

"It just got better."

Mac waved to someone, then grasped Cory's hand and held it. Another drum began its song, and Cory leaned over to Mac and spoke directly in his ear. "Do the Cree believe you can communicate with the dead?"

"I don't know."

"Find out when you're there."

"Where?"

"Canada. Go for it, Mac. You'll have a great time. I wish I had someplace where . . ."

He didn't urge her to finish the thought, but instead put his arm around her and pulled their chairs closer, and together they enjoyed the spectacle of music, dance, and color.

Sasha spent two hundred dollars on jewelry. All the way back to Summer she admired her purchases and described the beautiful things she hadn't bought. She attempted to clasp a silver necklace on Tony, but he gently pushed her away.

"Never," he said. "No jewelry."

"Sasha," said Mac in an accusing tone, "did you watch any of the powwow?"

"I certainly did. It was wonderful. Can't wait to go again."

Tony dropped her purchases one by one back into the bag. "You can't afford to go again."

The rain had ceased, the sky had cleared, and the moon was high overhead by the time Cory and Mac were parked alone in his driveway. Cory yawned and slumped in her seat. "I'm supposed to help Rob and his crew lay sod tomorrow. Five bucks an hour."

"Close your eyes and hold out your hand."

She obeyed. Something scraped against her palm as he dropped a light object into her hand. She looked. She was holding two silver web earrings.

"Remember when I met you?"

She traced the thin silver circle with her thumb. "I remember, Harvey MacNamara. I remember."

"Happy prom night, Cory K."

Another night ride through a maze of black highway and dark forest. Cory knew the route by heart, but as the road split open the wall of trees that disguised the familiar scenery, it was possible to imagine she was going someplace new, someplace unimagined.

The highway curved around a pond, and moonlight reflecting off the water half lit a solitary birch. Wind moved a pale branch. Cory saw the motion and her breath paused in her throat. It had seemed for that instant to be a ghost signaling, waving her down.

Cory pulled the car over. She looked across the water and identified the tree, an ordinary birch. "No ghosts," she said loudly. "No more ghosts tonight."

The stillness in the car weighed heavily. Cory reached and turned on the radio. It scanned until it found a clear-channel, far-away station. An announcer finished the Dallas weather report. "Ten-thirty," he said in a musty drawl. "Now here's a number to make you move." The song started and Cory's thumbs automatically beat out the rhythm on the steering wheel.

"Ten-thirty," she groaned. "I don't believe it — it's ten-thirty on prom night, and I'm headed to bed." She eased the car back onto the road. "No way."

A push on the accelerator, a crank of the wheel, and she reversed directions and sped back toward town. It didn't matter what Sash and Tony were doing. They would stop. It didn't matter if she woke Barb and Jeff and had to drag Mac out of bed. The night was not over. They'd go back to the café, load the juke with quarters, make some noise. It was prom night, it was spring, and Cory wanted to be dancing.